BENEATH THE CREOLE STARS

Albert Stanley Jackson

Copyright © 2025 Albert Stanley Jackson
All rights reserved.
ISBN:13-97989890432

Dedication

I dedicate this book to my father, whose unwavering love, support, and encouragement have been my foundation. Without his belief in me, I would never have found the courage to share my stories with the world. This is as much his achievement as it is mine.

LCCN-2025907365

Acknowledgements

I would like to thank Jack Rennekamp for his hard work on helping me with the cover design to Beneath The Creole Stars as well as all his hard work with formatting and editing.

I would also like to thank Jason Roberts for all his hard work with the editing of this book as well. Your help and advice are greatly appreciated.

New Orleans,
A City Where History
Dances With Mystery

New Orleans is more than just a city; it's a symphony of sights, sounds, and smells, a vibrant tapestry woven from its soulful music, the aroma of beignets, and the colorful architecture of the French Quarter. Wrought-iron balconies lean forward as if eavesdropping on whispered secrets, and the air hums with music, mystery, and life. Every corner of the Crescent City sings with excitement that is as intoxicating as the jazz spilling from a dimly lit club in the French Quarter.

Stroll beneath the warm, amber glow of the gas lamps as you feel the pulse of the city and experience the undeniable history that whispers of past legends. Feel its ghostly shadows that haunt dark alleyways. Listen as the festive, brassy notes of a marching band on Bourbon Street play mystical and rhythmic notes that seep into your mind, never to leave. Through the years, the city has become a place where ancient stones whisper forgotten tales, and the aroma of Creole spices blend with the scent of incense from dark and forbidden shops.

At the heart of this colorful mosaic lies Voodoo, a faith rooted in healing, community, and reverence. It has become integral to the spirit of The Crescent City, forming a symbiotic relationship that has thrived throughout the centuries.

The voodoo religion arrived in New Orleans with the transatlantic secondary trade. Though a shameful and dark part of New Orleans' history, these prideful people would not allow circumstances to shackle their spirits and interfere with their belief system. Faced with unimaginable hardships, these enslaved Africans wove their ancestral beliefs with Catholicism, creating a syncretic religion that thrives in the city's unique cultural environment.

Founded in 1718 by the French Mississippi Company, New Orleans rose from the swamplands to become one of the most culturally diverse cities in America. Its strategic position along the Mississippi River transformed it into a hub for trade and a crossroads for people from all over the world. French settlers laid its foundations, Spanish rulers left their mark, and enslaved Africans brought their resilience, music, and spirituality. Many diverse cultures intertwined over the centuries and with time, the practice of voodoo would incorporate Caribbean, Creole, and Native American traditions as well. Together, these influences fused into a cultural mosaic as rich and flavorful as the city's famous cuisine.

As a tourist destination known for partying and revelry, the lines between the sacred and the celebratory blur, creating an environment that captivates both locals and visitors alike. In a community as diverse as New Orleans, the line between the mundane and the mystical is as fluid as the Mississippi River itself. Beneath the bright lights of Canal Street and the haunting beauty of its above-ground cemeteries, you will find a culture where past and present become one, and the air feels charged with whispered secrets. The city does not just welcome you; it wraps itself around you like Spanish moss clinging to an old oak tree.

Voodoo is not just spirituality; it is performance art, history, and mystery all rolled into one. In secret candlelit ceremonies, worshippers call upon the Loas (Low-Ahs), powerful spirits who guide, protect, and sometimes demand a little rum or tobacco for their trouble. If you are lucky enough to witness a voodoo ceremony, you will feel the air thicken with each beat of the drums and hear reverent voices in song, pulling participants into a sacred space where the veil between the spiritual and mortal worlds grows thin.

No name in New Orleans Voodoo shines brighter than Marie Laveau, the 19th-century Voodoo Queen who remains a living legend. Equal parts healer, oracle, and humanitarian, this voodoo high priestess was known for commanding spirits with the grace of a maestro conducting an orchestra. From curing ailments to mending broken hearts, she served all those who sought her counsel. New Orleanians from all walks of life, both rich and poor, depended on and believed in her powers. Today, her resting place in St. Louis Cemetery No. 1 is a pilgrimage site, where visitors leave offerings and trace X's on her tombstone, hoping to summon a bit of her magic.

But Voodoo's legacy is not confined to cemeteries or historical accounts. It lives in the fabric of New Orleans itself. During Mardi Gras, the city's most exuberant festival, the influence of Voodoo is unmistakable. Beads and masks may dazzle, but behind the revelry lie echoes of ancient rites: offerings to ancestors, invocations of spirits, and the eternal dance between life and death.

To truly know New Orleans is to embrace its dualities: joy and sorrow, celebration and solemnity. Here, this ancient religion is not just a relic of the past, it is a living, breathing force that coexists in harmony, and where Voodoo remains a testament to resilience, community, and the enduring power of belief.

In this spellbinding city, where the streets whisper forgotten tales, every story pulses with a vibrant heartbeat, and every shadow holds a secret waiting to be discovered, reminding us that some tales are not meant to be understood, only felt and experienced.

The most unforgettable cities in the world are the ones that leave you forever changed, and if you are not careful, the sultry jazz, vibrant colors, and intoxicating aromas of New Orleans will cast upon you an inescapable spell.

The story you are about to read is fiction and plays into the Hollywood-esque perception of this noble religion. This tale is not meant to represent voodoo as it is known in New Orleans, but to play upon some of the rites and rituals that help make The Crescent City the enigma tourists are drawn to visit.

I hope you enjoy reading Beneath The Creole Stars and learning about the history and culture of New Orleans, a city that grabbed my heart and soul so many years ago, never to let go.

Introduction

The sharp bite of March night air cuts through my coat as I wait in this old New Orleans cemetery among the ancient cypress trees. This is not a place where anyone should find themselves on an eerily moonlit night, and yet here I am, caught in oppressive silence. With my stomach in knots, I wait patiently. The note she left insists we meet here this evening.

A beautifully exotic and mysterious woman whom I met only a few days ago, promises to share a voodoo ritual which will grant me what I seek, the understanding and ability to use dark magic that, until a month ago, I did not believe existed. Her letter demands I come alone and insists our meeting must take place in her family cemetery at midnight when her powers are at their peak. In past encounters, she explained hers is a religion that becomes stronger as time passes and that she must call on her ancestors' spirits to aid in the incantation, as bestowing gifts upon others is a shared and learned craft. For this particularly complicated ritual to succeed, she will need permission and approval from past generations of practitioners who passed their knowledge down to her. She promises that after tonight, both of us shall have what we deserve.

As I stand among the moss-covered vaults, a chill seeps into my bones. The wind howls, carrying ghostly whispers that slither around me. With nerves frayed, I begin to question my motivation for being here. Without warning, my knees buckle and I fall to the ground. Using a nearby gravestone for leverage, I pull myself upright and wipe these now slime covered hands on my trousers. Fear takes hold as I feel the damp ground beneath my feet shift, sending a sudden wave of panic throughout my body.

As if on cue, a figure materializes as the foggy mist rises from the ground. The silhouette of a woman slowly approaches, her features blurred. At first, I see nothing except a dark shadow, but as it draws closer, I recognize the middle-aged woman, her flowing white lace gown billowing in the wind like a ghostly shroud. The moonlight catches the fabric, creating a beautiful, mystical glow, a stark contrast to the dank despair surrounding us.

"Ma-Madame Celeste?" I stammer, my voice lower than a whisper.

The instant I recognize her, a gust of wind roars through the cemetery as the sky darkens above us, and heavy clouds move in to cloak the once-bright moon. She glares at me, her eyes aflame with anger and her silence more terrifying than any scream. Her hands move with practiced grace as she circles me, leaving a trail of coarse ash in their wake. Her voice rises in a haunting hum that chills my blood. From her other hand, flower petals drift down like macabre confetti, leaving a trail between us, as they flutter to the ground with a sense of foreboding. She takes her place six feet in front of me, and a visceral dread quickens my heartbeat. Her words sound harsh and angry as she continues to move with a sharp and aggressive swiftness. Though curious about this ritual, I battle with a growing sense of unease and cannot shake the feeling that something is not right.

Flames fly from her eyes as she raises her arms to the heavens, fury radiating from her. I have never seen such rage. A tempest of emotion swirls in her evil gaze as what I can only assume as hate and vitriol spill from her lips in an ancient tongue I am not meant to understand. Her practiced, guttural words and moans echo throughout the graveyard. Her gray beaded dreads whip around her shoulders as fallen leaves swirl around us into a chaotic vortex as the wind picks up.

The storm she conjures intensifies. Thunder rumbles with a sinister growl from the heavens, and with her next incantation, a bolt of lightning strikes a nearby ancient cypress tree, splitting it in two with a deafening crack. My heart races, pounding in my chest. I try to run, but my feet remain anchored in place. Paralyzed by an unnatural force, I feel something dark and evil taking a grip on my soul.

Continuing her chant, she beseeches the sky in a tone laced with more than spite. In it, you can hear the mournful cry of a broken woman. Her creole accented voice holds a deep, commanding presence and wraps around me like chains. I can only watch and listen as she continues with her methodical dance, hurling a cobalt blue vial in my direction. It falls to the ground, shattering at my feet. I want to look down, but I am frozen, ensnared by a horror beyond comprehension.

"All will be answered," she says as she slowly approaches, her voice a gravelly whisper which creeps into my mind.

"You wished to know about our heritage, our beliefs. Everything has a price, Mr. Ray."

As darkness and panic close in, my mind trembles in fear as I am about to become just another whisper in the wind, lost among these forgotten tombs.

Why I Became a Journalist

The memory of my mother's darkest day lingers like a haunting shadow. Living in a world filled with wonder and play, a young child rarely pays attention to the passing of days, weeks, or months. In the throes of childhood adolescence and too young to comprehend adult emotions, I failed to notice as my mother's heart grew heavy and dark with worry over the disappearance of her brother.

The average child measures time by the rhythm of their day. They know it is midafternoon as their body tires, and they realize they need a nap. Hunger pangs remind them that mealtime nears, and they protest as the inevitable frustration of forced bedtime looms. Without the prompt of pictures, I cannot recall my first three birthdays. I often question the memories that reside in my brain. Am I simply remembering familiar stories repeated back to me time and again, or are the pictures that play back in my mind uniquely mine? My first vivid memory I know to be my very own, occurred on March 13th, 1991.

That day starts like any other, with the comforting aroma of lunch filling our home. As I watch television, the familiar sound of Mom's humming drifts through the wall, a comforting melody I had not heard in months. The ringing of the doorbell shatters the tranquil moment, bringing everything to a sudden halt.

From the back of the house, I hear giggling and scrambling footsteps as my siblings, in a blur of motion, dash toward the door.

"I got it," mom cheerfully shouts, stopping them in their tracks as my brother quietly slides into my sister's back.

After wiping her hands with the bottom of her apron, mom answers the door.

A man in a dark uniform stands steadfast while clutching a white hat in his hands. The silence is heavy as he stands before mother, his eyes fixed on her before he takes a deep breath. Even as a child, I can sense something is not quite right as his voice shatters our peaceful home.

"Mrs. Schmitt?"

"Yes?" my mother replies, steady, yet apprehensive.

"Ma'am, I'm Officer Blanchette. I am sorry to inform you that the case regarding your brother Ray Lybarger has been closed." His words hang in the air, suffocating any remaining hope mother may have had that Uncle Ray would ever come home.

In an instant, mother collapses, her sobs echoing through the corridor. I want to rush towards her, but my sister's grip on my arm tightens. Her voice laced with concern, she whispers in my ear, "Mom needs her space,"

From that day forward, my mother rarely spoke of her brother, though the sorrow in her eyes was a constant reminder of the loss she carried. The police investigation may have ended, but the lingering uncertainty of his whereabouts prevents any sense of closure, as he will remain listed as a missing person.

The unspoken rule in our home was a painful one: There will be no mention of Uncle Ray's name. This was our silent vow to protect our mother from further grief. Over the years, I felt left out when overhearing whispers from my siblings, hinting of a mystery I am not meant to comprehend. Each time I dared ask, came the standard response all young children receive when asking certain questions, "You're too young, you wouldn't understand." This phrase always irked me beyond words, as I understood more about the world around me than I was being given credit for.

Having almost no knowledge of my uncle, the first piece of the puzzle would come during an interchange with my mother that, for most children, would have been a positive and prideful memory.

I was ten years old and eager to share my first A+ with mom. I remember holding the pages up and running into the kitchen.

"Mom!" I gleefully shouted. "Mom, I got my first A+!"

I received the grade for a story I had written in our creative writing class. On the bottom of the last page in red ink were the words I was so proud of; *you have the potential to become a talented writer.*

Mom took the pages from me and at first her expression was of pride and joy. In less than a moment, as she read the words of praise my teacher had written, the warmth in her gaze vanished, replaced by a cold fury. Tears welled up in her eyes as she crumpled the pages in her hand. Her frustration was evident in her furrowed brow and tight jaw, but I could not make sense of her response.

"I don't want you wasting your time on this kind of nonsense," she snapped.

The emotional roller coaster would end as I watched her tear the pages in half, as she uttered beneath her breath, "You're going to be just like your uncle, aren't you?" The sound of paper ripping echoed in my ears, and I could only cry as the story I had worked so hard on, like my heart, was being torn apart.

As the years passed, my mother's grief deepened, and she

turned to alcohol for solace. A common evening cocktail, 7&7, became her bittersweet remedy, while the shadow of Uncle Ray loomed larger, gnawing at her soul.

As I grew, so did my obsession with Uncle Ray's disappearance. During college, I stumbled upon an old article from the *Cincinnati Enquirer*, dated March 10, 1991:

Local Reporter Mysteriously Disappears

The community is on edge as beloved local reporter Ray Lybarger remains missing. Ray embarked on an assignment to cover the vibrant festivities of Mardi Gras in New Orleans, leaving Cincinnati on February 10. However, when he failed to return by February 28th, concerned colleagues raised the alarm, prompting authorities in both cities to launch an investigation.

Despite extensive efforts, no leads have emerged, leaving Mr. Lybarger's disappearance shrouded in mystery. Friends, family, and readers alike are holding their breath, hoping for news that will bring him back home. We will continue to provide updates as this story unfolds. We urge anyone with information to come forward. Any help from the public could make all the difference.

In that moment, everything shifted. I felt a calling to bring closure for my mother and our family. I decided to harness the energy for my joy of writing, and finally channel and focus it into a purposeful endeavor. I will become a journalist, like my Uncle Ray, with a simple goal of finding the answers to the mystery which has plagued our family for years.

My Career Begins

With my college degree in hand, I enthusiastically embark on my journey to become a respected investigative reporter, starting at the bottom and working my way up. I have meticulously planned my career path: I will build my writing skills, gain experience, and ultimately land a job at the *Cincinnati Enquirer*, my Uncle Ray's last workplace. Once I establish myself as a valuable and trusted member of the staff, I will approach the editor with the evidence I have painstakingly collected over the years regarding my uncle's mysterious disappearance. As my last name is Schmitt and his is Lybarger, my interest will seem purely journalistic, devoid of personal ties.

As I work to implement my plan, the echoes of Uncle Ray's story repeatedly play in my mind, urging me to unearth the truth before it fades into obscurity. The threads of fate are pulling taut, ready to unravel the mystery that has haunted our family for far too long. The clock is ticking, and with each passing day the pressure I place on myself grows. I must uncover the truth about Ray Lybarger's disappearance.

Driven by this hidden mission, I work tirelessly to carve out my reputation at the *Cincinnati Enquirer*. Each day intensifies my urgency to present my proposal to the editor. Both my stubborn German heritage and the gnawing fear of losing the chance to uncover what happened to Uncle Ray fuels my resolve. It takes longer than expected to establish my footing, but once I had, the moment I have been waiting for finally arrives. I choose to wait until the last day of the week to present my well-defined proposal.

As Friday afternoon rolls around, the office buzzes with a more relaxed energy, and I am hopeful our Editor-in-Chief will share this general sense of anticipation for the weekend. If things go south, and the editor refuses my presentation, I will have the rest of the weekend to reassess my life choices.

When the moment arrives, doubts flood my mind. Am I truly ready to put my dream job on the line for a debt of honor to my uncle? *Yes*, I tell myself. *Today is do or die. There is no turning back now.*

The Proposal

The *Cincinnati Enquirer*'s newsroom buzzes with the familiar hum of printers and soft shuffling of papers. Reporters answer phone calls and exchange hushed conversations, their urgent deadlines palpable. For five years, I have climbed the ranks here, all with a singular purpose: to solve a fifteen-year-old missing person's case. Two different police departments have given up on the unsolved mystery of the beloved reporter who vanished without a trace while investigating the vibrant, enigmatic culture of New Orleans. I, however, have not.

For years I have planned for this day. With the anniversary of my uncle's disappearance quickly approaching, the pressure mounts. I have decided I will not take no for an answer, and should my presentation fail, I may be looking for work come Monday.

Armed with a diligently researched proposal, I approach Editor Clarkson's polished desk. Palms sweaty and wrapped around a stack of old newspaper clippings and photographs, I lay them before him, noticing impatience in his eyes.

"Think of it as a tribute," I begin, forcing my voice to remain steady. "A fifteenth-anniversary piece on the disappearance of one of Cincinnati's reporters, best known for his comedic take on the travel industry and his interesting fact ladened articles."

Clarkson leans back in his overstuffed wingback chair. Fingers laced, brow furrowed and deep in contemplation, his expression is a mix of intrigue and skepticism.

"It just might stir interest at that," he muses, scanning the evidence I have collected throughout the years. His unexpressive gaze makes my heart race. Our frugal editor is notoriously known for his poker face during all crucial meetings where time away and the newspaper's money are concerned.

His silence is deafening as tension wraps around us, thick and stifling. Feeling he was losing interest, I need to bolster my case and mention the most recent thorn in the paper's side, our dwindling distribution rate, which has fallen steadily in the past two years. "You know we're struggling against the internet now," I remind him, desperation creeping into my tone. "This could draw in readers. Making this human-interest story only available in print form is certain to revitalize our readership. People cling to feel good stories like this, and limiting its availability will entice current subscribers and perhaps even gain us a few new ones. I promise this article will impress even you." I watch as the gears turn in his mind but doubt still hangs heavy in the air.

After what feels like an eternity, Clarkson's expression softens slightly. "Alright," he finally says, though his tone remains cautious. "You have my approval. I'll grant you access to the archives in the basement and an expense account for this story. Don't make me regret this decision."

A wave of relief washes over me, quickly tempered by the weight of what lay ahead. The stakes have never been higher, and uncertainty looms. As I collect my papers from atop his desk, a sudden rush of adrenalin causes a euphoric feeling to overtake my body. My years of hard work and planning have paid off. Our editor is still oblivious to the personal connection I have to this story, one that will help make this piece far more interesting than he or I can ever imagine. With his blessing and support, I am determined to unearth the truth that has remained buried all these years.

Presenting My Argument

With the newspaper green-lighting my article on Uncle Ray's disappearance, I am forced to reveal my long-held secret if I am to gain my mother's approval and cooperation. Hesitantly, she agrees to meet me at her favorite coffee shop in Cincinnati's Hyde Park neighborhood. I strategically choose a public place, hoping proper etiquette will ensure my mother's composure during this stressful encounter. Normally a woman of formidable presence and decorum, I cannot be certain of the reaction to the request I must ask of her.

The chatter of coffee shop patrons buzzing softly in the background mingles with the clinking of dishes haphazardly placed in the bus tubs near our table. Mother's perfectly manicured fingers lace around a hot cup containing a frothy cappuccino, her eyes desperately searching mine for a clue as to why I asked her here. I am about to disobey a long-standing rule. For years, Uncle Ray's name has been a forbidden whisper, his disappearance, an enigma buried deep within the family's history.

Taking in a deep breath, I begin, "Mom," the word catches in my throat.

"I must ask a huge favor."
Her expression shifts from curiosity to fright and disbelief as I explain my need to resolve this haunting mystery which has plagued our family for decades.

"To find Uncle Ray, I need his journal. It will serve as a roadmap and aid in determining my itinerary. I cannot leave Cincinnati unless I have insight regarding the last steps of his journey all those years ago."

She initially denies having any of his belongings, but I remind her I was in the living room watching cartoons that Saturday morning when the officers delivered two boxes containing the possessions he left behind in New Orleans.

After a hesitant sip of coffee, I continue as my voice trembles slightly.

"Mom, against your wishes, I have been researching his case. No one working for the *Enquirer* knows of the relationship between Ray Lybarger and our family, and I intend to keep it that way. I know it is a huge ask mom, but I need your blessing and approval so that I may study the evidence that was left behind in his hotel room. His journal will serve as an indispensable tool in helping me piece together the last hours before he came up missing."

My mother quietly listens in disbelief and before I can complete my rehearsed speech, she interrupts, commenting on my audacity to pursue this matter against her wishes.

"Mom," I implore, "I am determined to find out what happened to Uncle Ray. I hope to understand why he would disregard his family and put his life in danger."

The silence in the air between us grows tense. I shift uneasily in my chair, hoping I have not asked too much of my mother.

Several uncomfortable minutes pass before I sense an undeniable shift, perhaps even a flicker of acceptance, as she sighs deeply before reaching into her purse. She hands me a key affixed to a faded pink ribbon with only one tarnished key dangling from it. I slowly and gently take the offering from mom's hand and notice three faded numbers sloppily written on one side. Mother informs me it will open a lock to a self-storage unit by the CF Credit Union on the west side of town.

In her reluctance, I accept mom's unspoken blessing as a silent permission and perhaps a frail thread of understanding that the truth will finally find its way from the shadows.

The Storage Room

My emotions run high as I say goodbye and thank mom. I ask for a hug. She hesitantly obliges but it feels cold and distant. I am not at all happy with myself for upsetting my mother, yet I am elated that a new adventure is about to begin.

After a short drive, I arrive at one of Cincinnati's many self-storage facilities. During the trip, my mind races with thoughts of what I may find in the old abandoned boxes containing what remains of my Uncle Ray's life. Apprehension mounts and I heave a nervous sigh before getting out of my car. Using a poorly printed and smudged map from the office, I find storage unit 251.

My hands tremble as I fumble with the old padlock. Impatiently I wrestle with the rolling metal door before finally thrusting it upward.

Expecting a more well-lit area, I am not at all pleased that there is only one flickering fluorescent light illuminating the area. At this moment I am proud of myself for remembering to bring the flashlight from the glove compartment to help me carefully maneuver inside the unit. The room is nothing more than a dimly lit and musty cavern containing dust covered relics from years gone by. Spiderwebs shimmer in the flashlight's ray as I move it across the room. I cannot help wondering why mother is paying for this unit to hold only about five boxes, an old headboard and grandma's tattered old Chesterfield sofa. Becoming upset if anyone in the family mentioned Uncle Ray's name, my guess is that she did not want these items in the house as a reminder of his disappearance either.

With so few items in the unit, I immediately find the boxes marked "Ray." I stand above the cardboard containers in silence for a moment out of respect for my uncle. My heart races as I open the box closest to me. I am dismayed to find only clothing, a shaving kit, an old windup alarm clock and an item I thought had been lost forever, one of his trademark fedoras. The second box, however, reveals the treasures I seek. Uncle Ray's typewriter, reams of paper, countless pens, notepads, and the one item I hoped would finally answer the questions that until now have remained forbidden for decades, his journal.

From the box, I retrieve the only record left of Uncle Ray's life. I hold it tightly to my chest as I imagine him sitting at a desk, recording the day's events, or perhaps just a stray thought he did not want to forget. I take a deep breath and immediately regret it as the dank air filling this storage cube causes me to cough. Impatient for answers, I sit down on the old dust covered Chesterfield and firmly tuck the flashlight between my cheek and shoulder while lovingly running my hand over the leather-covered tome, which has gone untouched for years.

I feel my hands tremble as my finger glides along the spine

upwards towards a folded receipt being used as a bookmark. My mind races uncontrollably as I slowly open the book and inhale deeply; I have always loved the smell of the musty pages of an old book. Enthusiastically I immerse myself in his words, traveling beside him through the vibrant streets of New Orleans.

Each page is a revelation. Uncle Ray's fascination with the Crescent City is palpable, and his words paint images of Mardi Gras' chaos juxtaposed with the city's haunting allure. His entries are vivid descriptions of not only festive parades but also the excitement of Jackson Square, where artists of all kinds display their wares for all to see and purchase. He writes of jazz music filling the air as street performers entertain and enthrall the tourists walking by.

Reading further, I feel his awe, respect and the deep emotions he felt as he records seeing an unusually festive, but mournful event. "At first," he writes, "I thought it was yet another parade traveling down Esplanade. The loud brass horns played jazz music as lines of people danced with umbrellas, raising them up and down to the beat of the music. I thought it was a strange Mardi Gras krewe." He further writes how he had seen several parades, each krewe representing their unique history and themes. "This one is different," he continued. "Instead of a float there was an ornately decorated horse-drawn carriage. Two men dressed in black tuxedos, white linen gloves, and top hats, navigated the carriage carefully through the streets. The faded paisley curtains hang partially over the walls made of glass, slightly obstructing the coffin's view." He would later realize he had come upon something specifically unique to New Orleans, a jazz funeral. He wrote that, though he was glad to have witnessed such an event, he hoped never to again, as he experienced strange and uncomfortable emotions.

This would be the first of many oddities and unusual rituals Uncle Ray would discover as he delved deeper into the darker side of history that, in his opinion, made New Orleans one of the loveliest yet frightening cities he had ever visited.

The flashlight dims, prompting me to look down at my watch. I have lost all track of time. Mesmerized by Uncle Ray's thoughts and words I cannot believe more than an hour has gone by. I locked the storage unit, taking only his journal and the fedora with me. As my new adventure is just beginning, I cannot wait to read more about Uncle Ray's trip in my comfortable and brightly lit home.

Getting to Know Uncle Ray

Eager to dive into Uncle Ray's journal, I fix a quick sandwich and iced tea before adjourning to my recliner. Turning the lamp on beside the table, I adjust it to shine over my shoulder.

There are several entries which hint at Uncle Ray's investigative nature and the fact he was becoming bored with just writing about Cincinnati.

July 2nd, 1990
As a fledgling reporter for the *Cincinnati Enquirer, I've come*

to appreciate the unique charm of this city, which often flies under the radar compared to larger metropolises. While Cincinnati may not be as widely recognized for its theater scene as New York or San Francisco, it has its own character, shaped by passionate sports fans and the rich culinary tradition of its iconic chili.

As I navigate my role as a reporter for this newspaper, I am assigned stories about local crimes and the occasional sports victory, but I can't help but feel there's so much more to discover. There's something heartwarming about a city that blends the vibrancy of urban life with the intimacy of a small-town atmosphere, and perhaps that's why I choose to call Cincinnati home. Yet, I find myself unchallenged and unfulfilled. Our readers deserve to know what lies beyond the city limits. There are so many cultures in all the many cities and small towns around this country, I feel our citizens have a right to read about them from someone they know and trust.

As I read and carefully turn the worn pages, I find one of his last entries regarding his trip and thoughts on New Orleans.

February 2nd, 1991

It has been almost a year since my promotion to travel and leisure reporter. I have become weary of writing about cheap airfares and possible travel destinations, most of which I only know through exhaustive research and phone conversations with travel agents from those destinations. I must gather my courage and propose something fresh and exciting. With a surge of determination, I approached our editor with a bold idea for an article on travel, focusing on the local traditions and history of one certain city. I believe New Orleans to be a tourist destination which has the potential to truly inspire and capture the imagination of our readers.

As I step into my editor's office, my gaze is drawn to a delicate porcelain figurine perched on his desk. I recognize it from a story I did for school on voodoo and dark magic. I could be wrong, but the statuette resembles Madam Laveau, an iconic woman known to be the most famous voodoo High Priestess in Creole history. This moment sparks an idea, and I passionately

Uncle Ray records his experiences differently than I do, leaving me surprised to see he writes so formally. I was expecting a more relaxed approach to his journal entries. This reads more like a rough draft of a novel instead of the jotting down of notes and thoughts one would expect.

With my eyes growing tired, I decide my reading for this day has ended, so I place the journal carefully on the coffee table and prepare for bed. The day has been long, and with my head filled with Uncle Ray's vivid and picturesque words, I am certain any images that may dance in my head tonight will be colorful and entertaining.

Drawn from the depths of Uncle Ray's journal, the visions running rampant in my brain tonight are not at all what I expect. Instead of the joyous revelry New Orleans is known for, these hallucinations become a twisted descent into madness. This evening, sleep proves sporadic at best. What I thought would be pleasant and fun dreams become a surreal parade of images flickering as if from a broken film reel. At first, I find myself on Bourbon Street during Mardi Gras, surrounded by strange people in weird costumes, stopping to yell for beads being thrown from balconies. Surrounded by intoxicated and self-unaware people, I can hardly breathe and am only able to move in the same direction as the crowd.

The dream shifts, taking me to Jackson Square where the energy is palpable. As festive as other streets in the French Quarter, but not as crowded, a feeling of composed excitement fills the air. Finally, the festive picture of new Orleans I was expecting. Here there is so much to take in and enjoy. The sights and sounds of brass trios playing jazz music, jugglers, street performers who captivate their audiences with feats of magic, and so many other amazing acts. Together they all bring a calmer and more relaxing atmosphere compared to overly excited and inebriated tourists you may find on many other crowded bar-ladened streets.

I walk along the wrought-iron fence surrounding the park, where local artists proudly display their colorful paintings, and some are drawing portraits for onlookers. Things turn sinister as I approach a portrait artist. Her pastel coated fingers move swiftly as she creates her masterpiece. Curious to compare her work to the client who has chosen to have their face immortalized in chalk, I lean in closer. The likeness is uncanny, and I am impressed. Turning to examine examples of her art hanging behind her, my eyes follow the length of the fence. I do a double take, as one of the pictures now bears a striking resemblance to my Uncle Ray.

My heart pounds as I scan the other painting she has displayed. I watch as not only hers but all the paintings and drawings hanging on the fence morph into Uncle Ray's face, some weird and abstract, even Pacassoe-esque but most become morbidly dark images of Uncle Ray in various scenes depicting him in danger. Every painting I see becomes a blur, transforming into grotesque images, each one more disturbing than the last. In one, he is bound to a stake, flames consuming him as his facial expression denotes agony. In another, his head lay in a blood covered basket beneath a guillotine's glistening blade. As the nightmare escalates, a chill of despair overtakes me. I spring upright and an uncontrollable blood curdling scream breaks the stillness of my once quiet bedroom. Wiping my sweat covered brow, I attempt to slow my breathing. What I just experienced did not seem like just another dream, it felt as if I was truly experiencing these visions. In the back of my mind, I wonder what such dreams could mean. The images were so real I am forced to ask myself, *could this be a warning?*

In less than five hours, I am scheduled to leave Cincinnati. Getting upset and losing sleep is the last thing I want. Staring at the ceiling and half awake, I give up on getting more sleep and choose to stumble into the kitchen for coffee. With my cup of inspiration in hand, I decide to take another walk with Uncle Ray through his journal.

The scent of "old book" relaxes me and helps to settle my nerves. I open the journal and pick up where I left off earlier. The next few entries are innocuous. Uncle Ray writes about developing a taste for beignets and coffee, writing fondly of the Café Du Monde and how, in his opinion, there can be no better way to start your morning as a tourist in New Orleans.

The entries then take an ominous turn. He writes of clandestine meetings with enigmatic figures who whisper about a dark magic known as Voodoo, and ancient rites long since forgotten. I can almost feel his descent into the darker side of New Orleans' history. He writes about encountering shadowy figures lurking in dark alleyways and smokey jazz clubs where his ear would hear hushed talk of black magic, and someone named "Celeste."

I slowly turn the next yellowed page and find an old five-dollar bill with a single word scrawled on it. Again, the name "Celeste." I cannot help but notice his writing is not as neat as it is on the previous pages. It looks hurried and somewhat shaky. On the following page, he records a meeting with a middle-aged woman who claims to possess secrets unspoken and buried deep within the city. He notes her cryptic words regarding sacrificial rites which are performed to sustain power and protect those bound by this ancient magic.

His writing contains a mixture of intrigue and terror, yet I can also sense Uncle Ray's growing obsession. He has drawn a fragile line between fascination and fear.

Breathlessly I turn the page, and find his final entry, the ink smudged as if written in haste. He describes a midnight meeting, where a voodoo priestess was to reveal an ancient ritual, one meant for his eyes and ears alone. I hastily flip through the entire journal thinking I have overlooked or missed something. I can find no more information regarding his mysterious meeting, nor anything revealing the location as to where it was to take place. "Celeste, 12 am" are scribbled on the last page.

Those would be the final words Uncle Ray would ever record.

Hesitantly Hopeful

The flight from Cincinnati to New Orleans is more crowded than I had anticipated. As I navigate through the aisle and stow my carry-on bag in the overhead compartment, the scent of deodorants mingled with that of over-applied perfumes and colognes assault my nose and lungs, briefly taking my breath away.

Claiming my small seat, I attempt to shift into a semi-comfortable position as a sense of unease takes hold of my soul. After the bad dreams I experienced last night, warm overhead lights and the humming of the engines do little to relax me. I need a distraction, so I remove the latest copy of the Sky Mall magazine from the seat pocket in front of me. After the preflight safety demonstration, the plane finally takes off. Prior to storing my briefcase neatly beneath the seat, I remove my uncle's worn leather clad journal. Just the mere act of placing his words and memories on my lap brings instant relief from this stressful morning. Carefully I open the journal and take out my uncle's old press I.D. The sepia photo of him has faded but beneath the shadow cast by his trademark fedora, I see his eyes so full of life as they seem to stare back at me.

Over the course of the two-and-a-half-hour flight, my mind has more than enough time to envision distinct possibilities for how this trip might unfold. The first scenario involves a successful trip where I accomplish my goals, and a second, where I end up going down a rabbit hole from which there may be no escape. I fear the latter, as I cannot shake the feeling that Uncle Ray's disappearance is more than just an unsolved mystery.

The flight continues unencumbered until we cross into turbulent skies over the Mississippi Delta. My heart mirrors the erratic rhythm of the fuselage's shaking, as passengers' nervous whispers surround me. Suddenly, the plane rattles violently and the woman beside me goes into panic mode. She claws at the armrest and cries out. A flight attendant rushes down the aisle to comfort and reassure her, while the captain attempts to calm the rest of the passengers over the intercom. His voice is neither soothing nor convincing. As we continue to bounce through the unseen waves of air, I wonder if this is an omen, and perhaps a sign of things to come.

The rest of the flight is uneventful, other than the dramatically overwrought lady beside me who has decided to self-medicate with several rum and cokes. Not wanting to risk a drunk spilling alcohol on the journal, which is to be my roadmap and aid in finding out what happened to my uncle, I place it safely back in my briefcase.

We begin our descent towards Louis Armstrong International Airport and a sense of calm fills the cabin. Once on solid ground, I disembark into the vibrant chaos of an overcrowded airport filled with inebriated tourists who are eager to start their long-anticipated week of partying.

As I walk through the revolving door of the airport, I am greeted with New Orleans' infamously oppressive humidity, which envelops me in an unwelcome embrace. I feel my energy drain immediately, and I ask myself, *can you explain why you chose this time of year again?* In less than a minute, my white linen shirt transforms into a sweat soaked translucent second skin. A wave of embarrassment washes over me as I realize I have underestimated and overdressed for the sweltering climate of New Orleans.

I gesture to the next cab in line. Pulling up to the curb, the driver quickly starts loading my bags and I climb into the vehicle. As I lean back, the soaked shirt presses against my skin as it encounters the vinyl seat. "Oh man, that's cold!" I exclaim, expressing this unexpected but much welcomed relief from the summer heat.

"You alright?" the driver asks as he pulls away.

"Yes," I respond, "Please take me to the Place d'Armes (plass-darmz) hotel in the French Quarter."

Friendly enough, the driver tries to make small talk. But I quickly explain that the heat has drained me to the point of exhaustion, and I just cannot hold a decent conversation and wish for nothing more than to enjoy his nice, cold, air-conditioned car.

"Understood sir," he responds, "To the Place d'Armes it is."

I nod off during the ride to the French Quarter and what feels like mere minutes later; the cabbie announces our arrival.

"Well, here you are sir," he states as I exit the car. When I reach for my bags, the cabdriver insists on retrieving them himself, proudly proclaiming "This is what New Orleans' hospitality is all about." Frankly, I think he just wants a bigger tip, but who can blame him?

As he hands me my bags, I take a long look around and draw in a deep breath. The energetic sights, sounds and smells fail to rejuvenate me, and I sense something stronger than Déjà vu, a feeling I cannot properly put into words.

New Orleans is nothing like I expected. Though Uncle Ray

described it perfectly, I realize you cannot truly experience the Crescent City unless you have felt the energy and intrigue that help make the French Quarter so magical and unique.

I drag my mentally, emotionally and physically exhausted carcass to the front desk and inform them of my reservation under the name Eddie Schmitt. With minimal fanfare, I am handed my room key and given directions to the elevators. I find it curious that my cabdriver exhibited more warmth and kindness than the staff at this rather expensive hotel. As a result, I rush outside to add a little extra to the cabbie's tip, thanking him for his courtesy.

I will give props to the hotel staff for having the air-conditioning on full blast as I walk into my personal oasis. Leaving my bags at the door, I fall back on the bed and take a much-needed deep breath. Some Cajun cuisine and a restful night's sleep is what I need before beginning this new adventure.

What the Hell Just Happened?

I decide to unpack my belongings later as more pressing matters demand my attention. I step into a bathroom, which looks as if time itself has stood still. From the clawfoot bathtub next to the small shower stall and the pedestal sink, the space seems to whisper stories of past residents from decades ago. I snap myself out of my trance as I have a busy schedule and daydreaming will accomplish nothing.

Because time is a factor, I choose to shower instead of soaking in the deep and inviting tub. As I am here for at least two weeks, I will have plenty of time for a therapeutic soak later. As the hot water from the pulsating showerhead washes away the day's anxiety, I take this time to mentally prepare today's agenda. Feeling a bit peckish, I will stop at a nearby café for a quick bite and a rejuvenating iced coffee. If luck is on my side, the atmosphere will be conducive to studying Uncle Ray's journal, ensuring I do not overlook any details he recorded from his visit.

The French Quarter is famous for its lively atmosphere and delicious food, so I opt for a quaint coffee shop near my hotel. The front desk clerk raved on about the flaky croissants, whipped cinnamon butter and chicory-infused coffee they serve there, claiming them to be "the talk of the town." Her description of the place has me looking forward to every bite of pastry and sip of coffee. As the eatery is only a block and a half away, I choose to endure the heat and walk.

I arrive at the café' mid-afternoon, which appears to be the optimal time to grab a quick and refreshing snack. The place is sparsely occupied and pleasantly calm, the perfect backdrop for studying Uncle Ray's journal and contemplating my next course of action.

His last known residence was a boarding house in the Marigny, (Mare-a-knee) a neighborhood just on the outskirts of the French Quarter. Though Uncle Ray did not describe the house in specifics, he writes of the woman who ran the place in quite some detail. This is a recurring theme throughout Uncle Ray's journal. He often omits intricate details when describing buildings or places he may have visited. As a reporter he allows his camera to record details of architecture, statues and other physical beauties he need not immediately recall, finding that unlike people, these structures and art pieces never decline a photo op. He chooses to use his words to paint realistic portraits of the people he interacts with, making certain to describe in detail their features and colorful personalities. Of the last place he would ever reside, he mentions little except for the inconvenience of having to share a bathroom. He wrote fondly of a woman with unmistakable features, describing her as a tall dark-skinned woman with a bulbous nose, full lips, and hair neatly pulled into a tight bun, with an ink pen holding it tight.

Eager to investigate this place Uncle Ray wrote about fifteen years ago, I summoned a cab, taking the last drink from my iced coffee, and leaving half of my pastry on the plate. With hope and anticipation, I provide my cab driver with my intended destination.

The taxi ride allows me time to sort my thoughts, which have become tangled with excitement and apprehension. As we pull up to the address, I notice the boarding house has successfully weathered the test of time. Fine country craftsmanship and properly maintained, the old house stands as a relic of opulence amid modest surroundings. I am awed by the stunning architecture and intricate gingerbread molding. At the café I had read in a local real estate circular that the mansion was once owned by a very prominent and wealthy family who, as rumor has it, were heavy believers in voodoo and dark magic. With its history and wonderful curb appeal, I can understand why Uncle Ray chose this place so many years ago.

As I enter the boarding house, a bell jingles softly above me. To my astonishment, the woman from Ray's journal enters from the back office. I stare in amazement. She looks the same as Uncle Ray described, appearing untouched by time, down to the ink pen in her bun. I explain I am in New Orleans to write an article on the anniversary of the disappearance of one of the *Cincinnati Enquirer*'s journalists. When I present her with an aged black and white photo of Ray, I am surprised at her reaction. She instantly recognizes him as "Mr. Ray," recalling, "A very strange little man, but sweet and kind. He kept to himself mostly and didn't speak much with the other boarders."

I ask if she remembers the room he stayed in, and although she doesn't, she kindly offers to check her records. Dust dances in the air as she opens an old ledger dated February 1991. "Ah, there he is," she exclaims with a spark of excitement, "Room 4. Ray Lybarger." Curious to look inside and get a better feel for how Uncle Ray spent his last few days, I inquire whether the room is vacant. With a few clicks of the mouse, she tells me it is indeed unoccupied.

"Would you be thinking about renting the room?" she asks, her eyes sparkling with curiosity.

Not having considered spending my visit in the same room

where my uncle had gone missing, this question catches me off guard. I only wanted to take a quick peek inside. I have a lovely expensive room in the French Quarter, near everywhere I need to be during my visit here, and it comes complete with a private bath. Giving all that up seems absurd. Unable to stop myself, it feels and sounds like someone else answering, "Wow, that would be great!"

Showing extreme enthusiasm is one thing; whipping out my credit card is another. This all feels serendipitous yet frightening, and I must admit, I feel an unexplainable pull and connection towards this house. It is as though I am watching from above, with someone else footing the bill for the room. I am not one to believe in ghosts or paranormal phenomena, but could it be Uncle Ray guiding this incredibly stupid decision, or perhaps something far more malevolent at play?

My Last Night in the French Quarter

As I step out of the boarding house, a creeping sense of anxiety churns in my gut. What was I thinking renting that room sight unseen? Nostalgia, perhaps, a yearning to connect with Uncle Ray? No, those explanations are far too reasonable and measured, a stark contrast to the impulsive nature of my ill-advised choice. Truth is, it all seemed to happen before I realized it. I am a man of facts, not one to be swayed by superstition or whispers of the supernatural. Yet, the absurdity of it all gnaws at me. Somehow, I allowed my emotions to take the reins.

Unsure quite how it happened, I now must gather my things in preparation to leave this comfortable and plush hotel that is a jewel nestled in the heart of the French Quarter. Tomorrow I will leave the conveniently located restaurants, cafés and mysterious voodoo shops which beckon just outside the front door. It makes no logical sense to be changing addresses. With my expense account, I should relish my stay, not preparing to explain to the front desk staff at the Place d'Armes that I will be departing after only one night, instead of the two weeks I had reserved originally.

Later tonight, I will immerse myself in the intoxicating energy of the vibrant heartbeat of New Orleans, better known as the French Quarter. The hotel, with its myriad of amenities, has offered me comforts the boarding house will never match. As the afternoon wanes, for one last time I peruse the menus and tourists' pamphlets laid out invitingly on the table by the window. I daydream of all the meals and wonderful attractions that are nearby that I could enjoy during a stay here in the Quarter. Alas, for a reason I do not understand, I have chosen a pauper's accommodation instead.

For entertainment this evening, I plan to wander down Bourbon Street, where the sights and sounds promise to fill my senses with vibrant chaos, a welcome distraction before I drift into what I hope will be a peaceful sleep later tonight.

Neon signs flicker and buzz along the street, illuminating the many shops and bars in a kaleidoscope of color. I am surprised to see almost all the businesses have their doors and windows open, making certain those who pass by can see all the fun others are having. Their patron's enthusiasm flows out onto the street and is almost overpowering. An electric pulse reverberates in the air with an energy that words fail to capture. The street performers provide a backdrop of the bizarre and beautiful. Among them, the "human statue" stands immobile, a strange and brave figure, challenging onlookers to break his stoic facade. I marvel at his resolve, as I could never master such a task. Yet, it is the small black children tap dancing nearby that tug at my heart. Their clothes are ill-fitting, oversized, and the fabric thin and worn. Affixed to the bottom of their sneakers are old soda and beer bottle caps that clink with each step. How could I not drop twenty dollars into the old wooden cigar box they have placed beside their makeshift stage?

I imagine these children are doing their best to lighten their family's burden.

The French Quarter tonight is alive, throbbing with a vibrant energy that feels almost transcendental. The cabbie shared tales of bars that never close, and reveler's laughter echo all through the night. I had not considered how such a ruckus might seep into my dreams from all the late-night party animals, making the boarding house seem like a wise choice after all.

Having spent far more time touring Bourbon Street than I had planned, I find my way back to the hotel, the crowd's revelries still echoing in my mind. The night clerk at the hotel waves as I pass on my way to the elevator. I return her gesture in kind as I press the up button. Entering my hotel room for the last time, I look around at the wonderful amenities such as a blow dryer, a steam iron, and coffee maker, still not believing I somehow convinced myself to give all this up. *No sense in beating yourself up, the damage is done;* I think to myself as I adjust the thermostat.

After settling into bed and fluffing up the pillow just right, I reach over to turn out the lamp on the nightstand, and look back on my day, recalling the smells, sights, and sounds as they play in my head just before closing my eyes. Tonight, I hope to dream of jazz music and street performers, while boisterous laughter and images dance like shadows in my mind.

As my thoughts calm, the soft glow of light quietly dissipates behind my eyelids.

Change of Address

All packed, I hesitantly leave the hotel lobby of this lovely decorated and historic hotel. Taking one last look around, I heave a heavy sigh before exiting. In the sweltering morning heat of New Orleans, I further question my decision to leave the comfort of this lavish hotel for the rustic embrace of an old boarding house.

The cab ride through the French Quarter is uneventful, and upon arrival, the once inviting façade of the former mansion appears foreboding beneath the cloud covered skies.

The woman at the front desk greets me with a warm smile, her Cajun accent wrapping around her words with an inviting familiarity. As she hands me the key to room 4, she notes its proximity to the bathroom at the end of the hallway, as if that is a perk rather than an inconvenience. I thank her and make my way up the staircase, which leads into a sauna-like corridor where the humid air clings to me like an invisible shroud.

Using what looks like an old skeleton key I open the door. Upon entering, the room is stifling hot and uninviting. It exudes an eerie stillness, which becomes magnified with each footstep, as the floorboards creek ominously beneath my feet. Uncle Ray's journal described the room as quaint and homey, leading me to believe I knew what to expect upon entering. I could not have been more disappointed.

Sparsely furnished, an unsettling emptiness echoes off the plaster covered walls. An aged and ornate wardrobe exuding old world charm occupies one corner, and in stark contrast, a small chest of drawers sits haphazardly against another, its paint scratched and peeling. I look around for a closet and remember reading in a travel brochure that many New Orleans homes were originally built without that amenity; a fact I wish I had paid more attention to while preparing for this trip. I drop my bags on the blue velvet covered bench pushed against the footboard. Showing its wear and many years of use, a faded, and threadbare maroon paisley bedspread covers the full-sized bed. Directly across from the window housing the antiquated air conditioner is a desk, not quite large enough for a typewriter and notepad, feeling more like an afterthought than a workspace. A relic from another era, the window air conditioning unit wheezes and rattles, its ancient motor struggling against the humid air, in a feeble attempt to cool the room.

After unpacking my "unmentionables," I open the wardrobe, and the scent of mothballs greet me like an unwelcome apparition. I notice a small burlap bag tied with old twine nestled in the corner. *Must be Pot-Poruri,* I think absently, though an unsettling tug at my intuition suggests otherwise.

With no ice or soda machines in sight, I decide to venture out for a Styrofoam cooler and other essentials.

After shopping is done, my stomach reminds me I have forgotten to eat today. I stop at a nearby café which is devoid of

French Quarter charm. The Marigny is a small neighborhood and the locals seem to prefer an average aesthetic over opulence. Crowded and slightly noisy, I find a small table in the back, neatly tucking my shopping bags under the table, leaving just enough room for my feet.

My worst habit has always been eavesdropping, and I relish the chance to listen as a couple in their early fifties who are sitting near me conversing. They are discussing which walking tour they wish to take next. Another local couple nearby argues over who is paying for lunch. It is easy to forget that cities which draw a steady flow of tourism are also home to everyday hard-working citizens.

The server is accommodating and friendly as I order an oyster po'boy and beer. I enjoy the laid-back ambiance of this little café as I take my time and enjoy the delicious sandwich and refreshing beverage. While paying for my meal, I notice a small burlap bag identical to the one in my room displayed in a glass case at the register. My curiosity piqued, I ask the hostess what the mysterious item is, but she does not answer, as she becomes distracted by an inebriated patron barely sober enough to stumble out the door. As she rushes to help him leave, I shake my head in disbelief. I guess this is to be expected in a city where you can drink at any hour of the day. Realizing no answer is forthcoming, I pick up my bags and, just before exiting; I feel a tug at my sleeve as an elderly man leans in close. Softly he says, "gris-gris." (Gree-Gree)

"What?" I ask.

"Sit and talk with me here fer a minute, young fella." His voice is mysterious and intriguing, with a more southern than Cajun accent.

I accept his offer and pull out a chair next to him. I introduce myself, yet he does not seem interested in knowing who I am. He has information he wishes to share, and from his actions, he seems to want to keep it between just the two of us. He leans in close, his breath warm with the scent of chicory coffee, "gris-gris bags, they are used in voodoo for protection." he says in a hushed tone. His eyes widen as thunder rumbles outside. "Wherever you find those bags, there are spirits that need calming." He leans back and glances toward the door as if he is being watched and warns, "I've said too much," and with a wave of his hand, warns, "You best better go on now."

Bewildered yet intrigued, I signal for a cab as my mind races with questions. It has been an interesting outing, but it is time to return to the boarding house and unpack the amenities I picked up at the grocery store. I mentally scold myself for forgetting to purchase ice to fill my cooler.

Wet from an unexpected thunderstorm, I enter my room, which has reached a tolerable 75 degrees. The storm outside rages, mirroring the tempest of curiosity brewing within me. Unable to ignore it any longer and despite my better judgement, I remove the small burlap bag from its resting place in the wardrobe. I can no longer wait and need answers. I must learn about the contents and purpose of this item.

The stairs creak as I hurry down, clutching the small bag. Approaching the front desk, the woman's face drains of color as she gasps, "Mista', you better be puttin' that back where you's found it, right now!" She steps back, pressing herself against the wall as if the bag might reach out and ensnare her.

Frustrated and confused, I ask her what the object is and why she is so upset. She refuses to say more until I return the bag back to its resting place. I have never witnessed such an erratic reaction and find myself at a complete loss for words.

I take the bag back to my room and toss it on the bed. When I return downstairs for the answers I seek, I find she has closed the front desk, leaving only a sign atop the counter alerting guests and residents that "the office is now closed and will reopen at 6 am."

With more questions than answers, I angrily storm back upstairs. Before laying down, I return the bag to the bottom of the wardrobe and make a promise to myself to find out what this bane of my existence is. As I close my eyes, the old man from the café's ominous whispers play over and over in my mind. "Gris-gris bags… used in voodoo for protection… Wherever you find those bags, spirits need calming."

My imagination runs wild, wondering whether feeding my curiosity is indeed wise. Have I embarked on an adventure far more complicated than just retracing Uncle Ray's footsteps? Am I prepared to delve deep into a side of New Orleans most only read about? Did my uncle stumble upon secrets best left unspoken? And why and how was it he never came home? I have so many unanswered questions. Whatever occurred all those years ago, I am now more motivated than ever to discover the truth behind his disappearance.

Enjoying the Streets of New Orleans

In the darkness of this stark and uninviting room, unnerving nightmares swirl around me.

Unwelcome shadows dance in the night as soft undecipherable murmurs bounce off the walls.

A chill of unholy air brushes my skin.

My mind races as this night proves to be a restless one. I have never believed in things I cannot see, touch, smell, or taste. As a reporter, I base my life in reality and on facts, never being one to be swayed by the superstitious ramblings of others. But last night, something inexplicable happened, and I cannot shake the feeling that my uncle may have faced similar phenomena. I wonder, is that why some of his journal entries are so cryptic?

This morning, I am the first of the guests to venture into the communal bathroom, where a refreshing shower helps wash away the remnants of unease from last night. Dressed and in a much more social mood, I am ready to dive into the magical atmosphere only the French Quarter can provide. My research reveals two intriguing voodoo shops on Royal Street, and after breakfast, that is where I will begin my adventure.

As I stroll down Royal, the streets are surprisingly quiet for early morning, yet I am amused to see patrons staggering out of bars at 7 am, and equally astonished by the new ones sauntering in. I have heard whispers that each bar boasts its own signature Bloody Mary recipe, and I am tempted to investigate. Approaching the first voodoo shop, I am met with disappointment; it is closed, with hours posted from 10 am to 10 pm. I wander further down the street, only to find the second shop keeps the same hours. *Fantastic,* I think. *How am I going to kill three hours in the French Quarter?* Too much chicory coffee does not agree with my stomach, and sitting in a bar for hours does not appeal to me either. Just as I am about to let out a grunt of frustration, something catches my eye.

I cannot be certain, but it looks as if the street performer I noticed from last night is setting up his platform. Painted all in copper, he diligently makes certain a matching wooden box is level, as that is what he will use as his pedestal. He places an old top hat wrapped in copper foil in the corner of his stage to catch any tips those who pass by may bestow upon him. Once in position, this performance artist resembles any real statue one may encounter in any ancient city square.

Nearby, a woman arranges a makeshift table using sawhorses as a base. My curiosity piqued, I watch as she meticulously unwraps various sizes of brandy snifters, placing each one precisely where it belongs on a red velvet cloth which she uses to cover the plywood base. She has what looks like bricks wrapped in gold paper weighing down the corners. With exact precision, she fills each glass with a specific amount of water. I inch closer, captivated, as she focuses on the task before her. Still, unable to decipher what her talent may be, I position myself in front of her elaborate set up.

She double checks the small glasses and uses a wooden ruler to measure the water level of each. She then hides the empty boxes beneath the table, leaving the smallest out for tips, placing another brick in the bottom to keep the wind from blowing it away. With a spray bottle, she moistens her fingers and glides them along the rims of the glasses, producing gossamer tones that make my heart skip. She glances up and asks, "Do you have a request?"

Being the annoying person I am, I want to challenge her with a song I think will be almost impossible to play on something as simple as water filled brandy snifters. Searching deep, I locate in the farthest corner of my mind, a piece of music I detested as a child. The scourge of my twelve-year-old existence, "Für Elise." I remember the countless times Mrs. Buckly made me start over if I missed a single trill. I cannot begin to fathom how this young woman could ever play such a complicated composition on something as humble as brandy snifters, so I blurt out, "Für Elise!"

"Sure thing, mister," she replies with a smile, spritzing her fingers again before beginning.

I stand in awe as her hands dance across the glasses, her petite fingers creating a melody that is so beautiful I can hardly believe my eyes and ears. With each note, my smile broadens. She has replaced what was once an unpleasant childhood memory with one of renewed love for this song. I shake my head in disbelief and awe as I stroll away, slipping a ten-dollar bill into her tip box, not just for her amazing talent, but because she also answered the burning question: what on earth was I to do for the next three hours?

I head to Jackson Square and am surprised to find more street acts already performing. The entire square seems to dance to the beat of inviting music, as life is being displayed in the purest of living color. I am taken aback by the myriad of colorful acts, music, joy and laughter. I marvel that the cost of admission is always free to the onlooker to enjoy such a spectacle of art and self-expression. I want very much to visit the artists, but because of the dream I had the night before flying out, I refuse to go near the black wrought-iron fence covered in paintings that surrounds Jackson Square. I know it may seem childish to think it was real, but today, I do not wish to tempt the powers that be. Instead, I wander to my favorite act, the tap-dancing children. Not the same ones from last night, but just as talented, I deposit a generous tip before leaving and continue casually strolling through the square.

Stopping to listen to one last performance, I am disappointed when the leader of the reggae band announces, "We're going to take a quick break." As they leave, I retrieve my pocket watch and notice the morning has gotten away from me. It is 10:42 am and time to say goodbye to this vibrant street circus. I am in awe of the powerful energy that lingers in the air as I apprehensively walk away thinking, *I cannot wait to visit here again.*

The Gris-Gris Warning

Back on Royal Street, I head to the first voodoo shop on my list. A sign out front reads "Herbs, Spells, and More." The moment I step inside, a creeping sense of wrongness washes over me. The lights are harshly bright, causing me to squint, while sparkling clean glass shelves overflow with mass-produced trinkets and tacky figurines. The obnoxious scent of "pine forest" is so overwhelming that it elicits a nervous laugh from me as I think, this place is merely absurdity wrapped kitsch, and clearly nothing more than a tourist trap. I am the first to admit, I do not know what a voodoo shop is supposed to look like inside, but from what I have seen on television and in movies, even fortune tellers and tarot card readers shops are all dimly lit with a sense of mystique about them.

I pull the small burlap bag from my pocket as I approach the clerk. The naïve young woman launches into her rehearsed spiel, claiming the bag is a "Gris-Gris bag" meant to hold herbs and spices, promising to bring luck or love to its owner. Scoffing at its condition, she gestures toward a glass counter filled with similar items. Doing what any professional saleswoman would do, she attempts to make a sale by suggesting this one has long since lost its potency and I need to replace "that old ugly thing" with a newer and fresher one. She points towards her inventory of mass-produced Gris-Gris bags, each marked with tantalizing promises, all identical in appearance other than the labels. I ask to see one meant to bring wealth. She hands it to me, and I realize, with dismay, the fabric is merely a print meant to resemble burlap. Anger simmers within me as I shake my head. I can no longer tolerate the shameful attempt at authenticity surrounding me. I find it astonishing that tourists could accept any of this cheap merchandise as being authentic.

A short walk farther down Royal Street leads me to quite a different establishment. An old, weathered sign held up by rusty chains creaks overhead. It reads "Dark Lady's Potions and More." The words loom before me, the letters sharp, as if carved by a malevolent spirit. Beneath them, scrawled hastily in blood-red paint, a warning which sends a chill crawling down my spine: "Beware all those who enter Madame Claire's House of Voodoo."

I wearily peek through the cracked doorway. Once inside, the darkness is mystically overpowering and only faintly broken by the flickering glow of black and red candles, their flames dancing with a life of their own. The air is thick with the pungent scent of incense, wrapping itself around me like an unseen hand, beckoning me closer… and yet, something inside whispers for me to turn away. But I am unable to resist.

I slink in, encountering about ten brave souls who dared to enter before me. The entranced tourists hover around an elderly black woman dressed in a colorful smock, her head wrapped in a tignon (teen-yon). She warns her customers to tread carefully; and that touching even one of her sacred objects can bring extreme misfortune. My eyes adjust to the darkness replacing my initial fear with healthy skepticism, and I chuckle at her theatrics, dismissing them as mere showmanship, designed to extract money from unsuspecting visitors.

Her hands dance through the air as she recounts enthralling tales of ancient spirits that once ruled New Orleans. I feel a disquieting shift in the atmosphere as she blows the largest candle on the counter out. Tourists hang on every word, captivated by her dramatic gestures and the weight of her Cajun infused narrative. She insists they understand and accept that voodoo is more than talismans and trinkets. She states this is a religion but admits there are practitioners who have twisted its meaning and use it for dark sorcery, marring its reputation. Silently I sigh yet find myself oddly captivated and unable to deny the sinister thrill filling the air.

I back away from the crowd and lean against the doorway, observing as she fields absurd questions about dark magic and spells. She remains unruffled as she patiently answers each query, even the mean-spirited ones asked by young adults who wish to heckle her for a laugh.

"ENOUGH!" she shouts after a particularly rude comment.

"I will speak no more, but remember dear believers, some of dese items are not for da inexperienced."

I find this tactic to be ingenious. What better way to sell a product than to scare someone into buying it by warning them of the dire consequences of improper use? Yes, I have to say, she is exceptionally talented at her craft; her skill and showmanship are impressive.

After her patrons purchase their figurines, crystals, trinkets, talismans, and amulets, they scurry away, comparing their purchases with each other as they chatter on about the spells and dark magic the old woman spoke of earlier. I seize this brief peaceful moment to approach the strange and unusually interesting woman.

A wave of apprehension overtakes me as I cautiously introduce myself. I extend my hand, but she does not accept my gesture. Instead, her voice drops, sending chills through me. "I know who yuh are, young man, an' I know why yuh here. Yuh wish to uncover many things, but most important, yuh seek someone."

Stunned into silence, a sense of disbelief settles over me. I have seen so-called psychic charlatans on television, and if you study them closely, you can easily uncover their tricks. Her eyes, however, hold no deceit, only terrifying certainty. "C'mon, boy, dig into yuh pocket an' let me see it."

"See what?" I stammer, heart pounding.

"Madame Claire Voit has no time for games. De Gris-Gris boy, c'mon an' let me see de Gris-Gris." She holds out her hand, palm up and continues, "Yuh did bring it wit' yuh, didn't yuh? I have to say dat was a huge mistake."

With trembling hands, I produce the item I found in the wardrobe. Sufficiently terrified now, I am afraid to touch her hand and place the small burlap bag on the counter. Her eyes widen in alarm. "Oh dear," she gasps, the worry clear in her voice. "Dis is not good, young man."

Confusion engulfs me as I stand there, lost for words. "It all comes full circle," she continues, her cryptic statements igniting my frustration. "But I never thought I would see de day."

"Look, lady…."

"It's Madame Claire to yuh boy, best yuh don't forget that."

I open my mouth to protest, and she interrupts, raising a hand to silence me.

"An' before yuh speak further, I muss reveal truths yuh may not wish to hear."

"All right, *Madam Claire*," I pause, as being chastised like that by someone I do not know irks the living crap out of me, "I just came to ask you about this… whatever it is. I found it at the bottom of a wardrobe in my room at the boarding house where I am staying. It is the same room my uncle occupied fifteen years ago. I am not here for theatrics or stories. I am in search of answers. Your shop appears authentic and true to your religious practices, and though I do not believe in the supernatural, spells or rituals that I have heard are associated with the occult, I do think you might be the only one who can convince me otherwise."

"yuh would do well to remember manners an' respect. If yuh are to find de answers yuh seek, yuh muss understand more 'bout our religion an' de craft. Yuh need to be returnin' dis to its place," she insists, her voice sharp. "De longer it is missin', de more chaos, de spirit will unleash."

"I don't understand," I reply, my frustration bubbling over. "I mean no disrespect, but I am a nonbeliever in all this voodoo stuff Madam Claire."

"Dat's better," she says with a crooked smile. "Dis, my boy, is a Gris-Gris, an' not jus' any Gris-Gris. Dis one has been prayed over by a powerful voodoo priestess. Each family has deir own way of preparing dem. Yuhs see dis blue twine?" She asks. I nod yes. "Dat is da mark of a very powerful voodoo priestess, an' I've not seen her work for years. It was placed dare to help keep a very angry spirit at bay. Story is, a young man came 'round curious about de darker aspects of dis city. I believe yuh know who I speak of. A nosey stranger, a reporter who ask too many questions an' dug too deep. One who paid for his deceit an' hubris."

Her words echo in my mind, and the truth settles like ice in my veins. I am stunned speechless. She seems to know so much about why I am here. Now, understanding what Uncle Ray was trying to uncover, I must read his journal with a fresh set of eyes and a clear and accepting state of mind. I overlooked most of what he wrote regarding voodoo and dark magic as mere sensationalism and possibly the ramblings of a man on the verge of a breakdown.

"Now go," she orders, her voice a low rumble. "Put dat back where yuh found it. De spirit's wrath may already be upon yuh."

"Wait!" I cry, but she cuts me off.

"Meet me at de Jazz Note tavern on Carondelet at midnight an' have a red wine waitin' for me."

"That's too late," I protest.

"Do yuh want answers or not boy?" she retorts. "I can't make it earlier den dat as I have to have time to close shop, don't I?" She turns to restock the items purchased by the tourists earlier and dismisses me with a wave of her hand.

"Yes ma'am, midnight it is," I say, while thanking her for her time.

I shake my head in confusion and disbelief of all I have heard and seen. I exit her shop and immediately flag a cab down to get the small burlap pain in my ass, back to the boarding house as soon as possible.

The Late-Night Meeting

The moment I step into the boarding house, Ms. Nahomie lambasts me for disturbing all the other boarders in the house. She claims a great deal of noise was coming from my room all day. I try to explain I have been in the French Quarter all morning, but my words fall on deaf ears. Her tirade comes at me fast and furious, her gaze sharp as a blade.

I take the scolding in silence, keeping my head down, knowing better than to argue. After she has had her say, I retreat upstairs, my stomach twisting, not knowing what condition my room will be in, but I am about to find out.

When I open the door, chaos greets me. My heart sinks. Every drawer in the small dresser is yanked open, and all my clothes are scattered across the room as if a tornado came through. The chair belonging to the small desk is overturned, and the lamp from the nightstand crashed onto the floor, its broken glass glistening in the sunlight.

There is no mistaking it. Something, or someone, was undeniably here, stirring up trouble, and now a chill runs through me. I know what I must do first, immediately place the Gris-Gris back where it belongs, hoping its presence will calm whatever restless force or forces are at play.

In the over thirty minutes it takes to undo the damage caused by what I can only assume is a mischievous spirit, I sit on the side of the bed and try to convince myself this never happened. I survey the room, glad the only true damage was an old lamp, and then something catches my eye. One drawer on the lowboy will not close properly. I try to push it back in, but it will not stay, as if something has fallen behind it. Exhausted from the struggle, I give up on the drawer; its persistent refusal to close has finally worn me down.

With the arduous task of cleaning complete, I need to regain my energy. Beef jerky and a warm soda from my cooler will have to suffice, as I cannot summon the energy to venture out for something more nutritious. I must build back strength before my rendezvous with Madam Claire.

I set the bedside clock for 10:30 pm, and lie down to nap, praying this rest will settle my nerves.

The alarm goes off and I find myself woefully unprepared or motivated for the midnight meeting. My head is pounding, and I feel half-dazed, but there's no time to waste. I silently slip out of the boarding house, stepping gingerly to avoid drawing attention to myself. The last thing I want to do is alert Ms. Nahomie to the fact that I am leaving. I have had enough of her chastising me for one day.

I slip out into the night, the silence broken only by the restless crickets chirping. Humidity hangs in the air as the moon casts a silver glow over Carondelet Street, its light dancing off the wet pavement. It is an uncomfortable walk, each step heavier than the last. My mind races full of questions. I cannot help but wonder, what does Madam Claire know about my uncle's disappearance and why did she insist on meeting me in a bar of all places? The anxiety pooling in my gut only festers as I grow nearer the Jazz

Note Tavern.

As I enter, there is an unexpected and muffled calm. The place is quieter than I imagined; the low hum of conversation is barely audible over the smooth, soulful saxophone solo that is drifting from the corner where the juke box draws a small crowd discussing which songs would be played next. A palpable sense of mystery fills the space. The atmosphere is deep, intimate, and unsettling. The bar is surprisingly crowded for this time of night and buzzes with an energy I hadn't expected. The clientele is also different from what I'd envisioned. Couples sit close together, leaning into each other, their faces aglow, lit only by a flickering candle in the center of their table. I immediately feel out of place and uncomfortable.

At the bar, I order two red wines and find a spot near the door. Every eye in the place follows me as I walk to the table. Nerves sufficiently shot, my hands quake as I set the two glasses of wine down, glad to have made it on time. I already know it to be a mistake to disappoint Madam Claire. Each minute I wait feels like an eternity.

She enters, and it is as if her appearance was expected. The room seems to hold its collective breath. Like a chilling shadow, her reputation seems to proceed her. I barely recognize her at first. She is dressed in casual street clothes. The absence of her colorful smock or Tingen head wrap makes her look ten years younger. Her presence, however, is undeniably commanding and fills the bar with an almost magnetic force.

A collective gasp is loud enough to be heard above the music, and the chatter dies, as if some invisible force gave a command. The jukebox stops playing mid-note, as the patrons remain frozen in time.

It's as though everyone in the room is waiting for her permission to continue the night. Their heads turn, following her every movement. Noticeable fear, respect, and perhaps something darker are all wrapped up in their gazes.

Her silvery, almost blue dreads cascade down her back, and with each step she takes, the beaded locks click against one another in harmony. I watch in stunned silence as every person in the room, without exception, falls silent.

I rise instinctively, pulling her chair out for her as she approaches our table. She sits without a word, and with that simple act, the club's ambiance returns, as if nothing ever happened. But I remain stunned. What was that? Were they in awe of her... or afraid?

"Merci, for de respect yuh show…an' merci for da wine," Madam Claire says, her voice smooth but laced with an underlying sharpness.

I nod, eager yet nervous, my mind racing with questions. But I wait, knowing she's the one in control here.

"Listen well, dear," she continues. "I wanted for to meet y'all here for two reasons. First, to see if yuh serious 'bout 'learnen what happen to yo uncle. An' second, to see if yuh have learned some respect."

I shift uncomfortably under her gaze, feeling small despite my height. I swallow hard.

"A place like dis," she gestures at the surrounding patrons, "Ain't da spot for da deep conversation we need to have. An' as yuh can see, I make these folks real uncomfortable. I'll explain more when we meet again."

"Meet again?" I question.

"I thought you were going to tell me tonight…"

She raises her hand to stop me from saying more. I cannot help but feel slighted as she demands respect from me but shows very little in return.

Her eyes narrow slightly.

"I need yuh to meet me on Sunday noon, at Woldenberg Park. We got a lot to talk 'bout. Yuh got any personal things from yo uncle? Yuh bring 'em wit' yuh. An' I want yuh to learn 'bout our way of life, our religion, the true meanin' of voodoo. Not da foolishness people talk 'bout in the movies, but da real thing. Da history, da power, how it connects to our families an' lives. Yuh need to understand what yuh 'bout to get into. Yuh are gonna learn things not many of yo kind ever will. I pray yuh ready for what yuh will see, an' dat yuh accept da truth, no matter how hard it might be."

She pauses, watching me closely.

"I'll have books delivered to da boarding house in the next day or so. Study dem. An' study dat diary from yo uncle, yuh read dat too. Yuh got tree days to prepare dear, tree days."

I nod, though my heart is hammering. She is not asking me to just listen, she is asking much more, she expects me to believe and to understand a truth I am not sure I am ready to accept.

She continues, "There are things I wish I didn't have to tell yuh, but I muss. Yuh seem like a good boy, an' I don't want no harm to come to yuh. But dis road yuh walkin' down…it ain't one to take lightly."

She stands, and before I can offer to help with her chair, she raises a hand, stopping me.

"Oh, don't worry 'bout pullin' out my chair. Yuh has already shown me respect. Merci for da wine, an' I wish yuh a good night, dear."

And just like that, she is gone.

The bar falls silent again as she exits, and the moment she clears the threshold, it is as if she were never there. Everyone returns to enjoying their evening. All except one. Someone who feels the need to interject himself into my life.

A middle-aged man rushes to my table, startling me. His voice is low and with some urgency, he asks.

"Do you know who that was?"

He gives me no time to answer.

"That was Madam Claire. You don't take her lightly, boy. She's not someone you trifle with. Anything she shares with you... keep it to yourself. You don't want to know what happens when someone crosses her. Trust me, the last person who got curious about her family... well, let's just say they won't be asking anymore stupid questions."

I swallow hard, my pulse racing. The weight of his words settle heavy in my chest, a greater sense of foreboding I have never felt.

Something tells me I've just taken my first step into a world that will forever change the course of my life.

The Notepad

At two o'clock on this cloudy New Orleans morning, the streets are unusually quiet, the only sounds are a barking dog and the distant clang of church bells. The humidity has subsided, leaving the air crisp and cool as I make my way home. But something else is different, a subtle tingling of my skin. A discomforting feeling hangs over me, one I cannot shake. I think I am being followed.

A black bird circles overhead, cutting through the dimly lit sky. It disappears in the darkness, only to return minutes later, wings spread wide as it glides just above my head before flying off again. The pattern repeats, as if the bird is deliberately harassing me. He is not being aggressive, just acting odd and disturbingly persistent. I snap my mind back to reality and continue to make my way back to the boarding house, blaming the three glasses of wine I had earlier this evening for my overactive imagination.

I reach the front door at 2:30 am, and feeling relieved, slip the key into the lock. Silently I make my way upstairs, hoping not to disturb anyone. As I change into my pajamas, movement from outside the window catches my eye. The black bird has followed me home and is now perched motionless on the windowsill. Can this be real? But there the little bastard is, staring at me through the glass with an unnerving gaze, its dark eyes focused and unblinking.

It can't be the same critter, I tell myself, *just a coincidence*. To ease my mind and put the walk home behind me, I draw the drapes shut. I cannot allow my hyperactive imagination to keep me from the sleep I need.

The harsh brassy ringing of the alarm causes me to jolt upright from the bed. With a quick slap of my hand on top of the clock, I reach for the aspirin bottle to deal with my slight morning headache. I pull open the curtains and two things draw my immediate attention: the drawer that refused to close yesterday, and the same black bird still perched on the ledge of the window. I tap the windowpane, hoping to scare the flying rat off, but it doesn't budge. Last night, the darkness hid the bird's identity, but this morning, a slight cock of his head and defiant posture confirms my suspicions. He is a crow alright, and I know them to be notoriously stubborn creatures. "Fine," I mutter, "You can stay. It's not like you're bothering anyone."

But the drawer... that, is annoying me. The last thing I need is for Ms. Nahomie to deem the unit broken and charge me for a new one. With a sigh, I take my socks and t-shirts out, and remove the offending drawer, hoping to repair whatever damage that may have occurred from my spectral visitor yesterday. I set it on the floor and feel around inside to check if the track is secure. Perhaps in my haste I did not align it properly. Feeling around, my fingers brush against something strange in the back of the cabinet.

I jerk my hand back, heart pounding. It does not feel like the small burlap bag I found in the wardrobe. I cannot discern what is there, and the dim light provided by the overhead light fixture is not enough to help me see clearly. With the luck I have had these past few days, I am not stupid enough to stick my hand back in there again without a flashlight.

Could it be yet another voodoo charm or talisman? I cross my fingers, hoping that is not the case. In a state of angst, my stomach churns.

To be safe, I slide the drawer back in place and walk away, my curiosity battling with my better judgment. Like a needle stuck on a record, playing repeatedly in my mind is the phrase, "Something is in there." I try to ignore it, but it gets louder as the minutes tick by.

What's the worst that can happen? I try to convince myself.

Against my better instincts, I yank the drawer out again. With a loud thud, it hits the floor. I am determined now. Hastily, I reach inside, making things worse for myself. As my fingers brush up against it, the object slides further down to the next drawer, just out of reach.

"Damn it," I mutter. "This is ridiculous."

I pull out the next drawer, plopping it on top of the first. Finally, it is visible, the annoying object causing all this drama. A wave of relief washes over me as I see only a small, unassuming notepad. An innocuous find certainly, but then, for a moment, I feel a rush of unease, perhaps a premonition.

I remove the pad now resting on top of my socks. It is smaller than a spiral bound notebook but not as large as a journal.

And then I see them. Letters written in red ink, R.A.L.

My heart skips a beat. Those were my uncle's initials.

This is no coincidence. My mind races. What was my uncle's notepad doing tucked away in the depths of an old dresser? A strip of yellowed Scotch tape marks the cover, its edges cracked and curled; a clear sign it has lost its adhesion during the pad's long residence as it was taped to the back of the cabinet. What could be so precious, so closely guarded, that it demanded such a secretive hiding place?

My hands tremble as I flip through the pages, and my breath catches in my throat. The handwriting is unmistakably Uncle Ray's.

But the questions flood in. Why would he hide this? Why keep such a strange, private record? The words scrawled on the pages create a disjointed, almost fragmented feeling. In complete contrast to his journal, this is not how Uncle Ray writes. The sentences appear to be scattered thoughts, which only spark more confusion in my mind. One name stands out, Saphron Mink. I recognize it from his journal. But he never wrote much about her. Could this be an addendum to his research, some secret notes he did not want anyone seeing? I continue, unable to help myself.

I keep reading, even though a voice in the back of my mind tells me I am trespassing on something far more personal and that I should stop now. But his words, they pull me in. And what I learn next is something I can never forget.

It seems Uncle Ray's interest went beyond the rich, historical culture of New Orleans, even deeper than the festive French Quarter and this city's colorful art and music scene. He had become obsessed with far more than just the religious history of voodoo; he had become entangled in its darker side, which is steeped in magic and secret rituals that promise power, control, and even revenge.

My hands shake as I read a passage: "Saphron has taught me some things, but there remains so much more I want to learn. There are incantations for everything: revenge spells, healing spells, and even ones to make people love you. Before I leave New Orleans, I must learn a revenge spell and how to use it on Michael when I get home."

I am forced to stop reading as I ask myself, "Michael? Who the hell is Michael?"

This is too much. More confused than ever, my mind races, leaving me unsure of what to believe. As I close the aged cover of the notepad, an unsettling thought creeps into my brain. Learning about this uncle, a near stranger, is proving far more involved and intense than I ever could have imagined.

This notepad provides more than just a glimpse into a forgotten corner of my uncle's life. It serves as a warning. In New Orleans, magic lives beyond myth and legend. It can be heard in their vibrant and soulful music. Looking deeply enough you can see it in the colorful and inviting citizens who reside in this city. It pulsates in the streets and through the very air you breathe. Once you start down that path, in search of the illusive magic, even unwittingly, you may find yourself unable to turn back.

And that black bird sitting outside my window? Why suddenly has he shown up? I'm wondering, can it be an omen? Could it be a warning sign one may not notice until it has become too late? I remember the raven in Edgar Allen Poe's poem. Am I about to regret putting my investigative nose where it does not belong?

With no way to find the answers at this time of night, I decide to prepare for bed. Madam Claire has promised to send over books which are sure to answer most, if not all these relentless questions occupying my mind.

Class is in Session

Every morning begins the same way. I wake in this godforsaken room, drenched in sweat as if I have been wrestling with the weight of the world while I slept. Yawning, I try to shake off the remnants of another restless night. Not entirely awake, my blurred vision focuses on a neatly folded piece of paper tucked under the door. *Now what does she want*, I think. I am certain the note is in response to my having to ask for another lamp for the room. The correspondence will most likely inform and regale me with a tale of the broken antique lamp's unique history and emphasize its irreplaceable nature. It may be necessary to visit a bank to obtain a small loan to cover the damage caused the other day by what, or whoever, trashed my room.

Not wanting to start my day in an angry mood, I leave the note folded and unread, tossing it on the small desk. I glance in the mirror above the desk and barely recognize the man staring back at me. A few gray hairs have sprouted at my temples, a new crease between my brows, and dark bags under my eyes reflect a life unraveling. I lean closer, squinting, as faint echoes of recognition tug at me. Running my fingers down my cheek in disbelief, I realize I look as if I have aged ten years in less than a week.

The man in the mirror no longer looks like me, yet somehow feels so familiar. Then, as if the universe has aligned to bring me understanding, a beam of sunlight pierces this gloomy room, illuminating Uncle Ray's journal on the desk. I flip through the brittle pages until I come to the old black and white photo of him. *Why hadn't I noticed this before?* My uncle's likeness stares back at me. We share the same jawline and eyes, tired yet still full of wonder. Looking further, our noses are also identical. The only difference between him and I right now is that I am not wearing his favorite fedora. *What the hell? This can't be real.* Just two days ago, I didn't look like this. How could my face age nearly a decade in just days? Sure, I've lost countless hours of sleep trying to unravel the mystery of what happened to Uncle Ray, fueling my nights with coffee and sleeplessness, but this … this is not right.

In disbelief and perhaps denial, to maintain my sanity, I tear my gaze from the old photograph and glance at the window. Perched silently on the sill is the crow, its presence marked only by the occasional quiet rustling of his feathers. Its eyes, like shiny black beads, relentlessly watching. I wonder what he is waiting for, leftover crumbs from a pastry, or something more ominous?

Shaking off the unease, I force myself to confront the note I have been ignoring. Written in an elegant script, it reads: "A delivery has arrived for you at the front desk. Please come gather your things; they are taking up valuable space." After a quick shower, I head downstairs, unprepared for what awaits me. I freeze in my tracks, eyes wide in disbelief. Madam Claire promised delivery of a few books. I was not expecting the entire Loyola University Library. Ms. Nahomie, arms crossed and eyes blazing, orders me to remove the books immediately.

My first thought is, *I'll need a wheelbarrow to haul them all upstairs.* As I struggle with the last armload, dread settles in. *So…* I ponder, *Where exactly am I supposed to put all these books?* I collapse onto the bed, the pile of literature spilling around me. Looking at the many colorful covers, I wonder which book to start with.

The answer comes as I notice Madam Claire's thoughtful preparation, which removes any guesswork. Small round stickers adorn each book, all numbered. A creeping unease washes over me. She has a carefully outlined agenda, one designed to guide me through this maze of reading material. This woman has set forth a lesson plan; a meticulous labyrinth deliberately meant to manipulate and lead to one specific conclusion.

I gather the books in sequence and open the first one. As I do, a slip of paper flutters to the ground, the handwriting hurried but legible.

"Voodoo, dear, is a complex and multifaceted religion."

In larger print, she emphasizes, "Now remember, above all, we are learning about religion here. It encompasses a wide range of beliefs and the connection between the physical and spiritual worlds. We seek to live in harmony with the spirits and nature. Our religion emphasizes balance, reciprocity, and respect. It is not just about uttering spells and rituals, but a deep connection few can understand. There is a symbiotic relationship between voodoo and New Orleans. In the strictest sense, one cannot flourish without the other."

I spent the next three days in coffee shops and quiet café's pouring over the history of the religion known as voodoo. There are many facets which make it a one-of-a-kind belief system that most, including myself, brush off as hocus pocus. I initially dismissed it as superstition, pure sensationalism. These spells, and rituals seem designed to instill fear, but also hope. Yet I learn it runs far deeper and is much more complicated. Certainly incantations, talismans, and rituals are part of the ceremonies as they all serve a purpose: to connect with the Loa, who are intermediary spirits that act as conduits between the human and divine realms.

I am shocked to find there to be such a strong relationship between Voodoo, Catholicism, and the Crescent City. I learn how saints intertwine with the Loa, and prayers merge with invocations. Over many years, they all have grown and become unified with the deep historical roots of New Orleans.

I read on and focus on the Loa's I believe to be most important.

Legba, depicted as an elderly man, closely associated with St. Peter, opens the way for communication with spirits.

Erzulie, the Loa of love and beauty, is linked to the Virgin Mary, known for her compassion.

Baron Samedi, a skeletal figure in a top hat, is the grim reaper of voodoo, associated with St. Expedite.

Lastly, Damballa, the serpent Loa of fertility and wisdom, often equated with St. Patrick, is a representation of creation that defies the typical evil associations of the snake.

This fusion breathes life into the city in ways I never imagined. With my eyes now open to the wonders of her way of life, my heart embraces the mysteries I once dismissed, feeling a sense of awe and hope that she indeed is the one to help me find my uncle.

My brain aches from the constant flow of information I have ingested these past three days. As I devoured all the knowledge she provided for me on this new faith, I am mentally, emotionally, and physically exhausted, leaving me in dire need of rest.

Tonight, I must sleep. I have pushed myself too hard and the meeting with Madam Claire tomorrow must go well. Therefore, it is paramount that I arrive with a sharp mind.

After turning off the lamp and settling in, I cannot ignore a strange consciousness overtaking the room. Shadows creep along the walls as eerie chills slither up my spine.

The crow is still outside my window, his eyes locked on me.

And the whispers begin.

As I try to sleep, faint murmuring and distant voices reverberate throughout the room, in a foreign tongue I cannot understand. They grow louder as spectral images dance across the ceiling.

I close my eyes tightly as I try to shake off the unease. *It's just my mind playing tricks,* I tell myself. But deep down, I know something, or someone, is trying to reach me. Are these spirits here to warn me? Are they watching over me? With all I have read and learned, it could be one of many possibilities and I will not know for certain until I speak with Madam Claire.

Questions swirl in my mind as I drift off to sleep. Though I cannot understand them, each muffled voice seems to echo promises of revelations yet to unfold. A sense of calm overtakes me and this evening, I get the much-needed rest that has eluded me these past several nights.

The Park

After several days of diving deep into the myriad of books Madam Claire left for me, I can use a day off. I have a storm of questions churning in my mind, but one looms above all others. Why has this crow adopted me and why does he follow me everywhere? This morning, I stepped into the French Quarter, craving a simple breakfast of four beignets and a steaming cup of coffee. Over my left shoulder, perched atop a lamppost like a feathered guardian, is my uninvited companion. Not wanting my new pal to go hungry, I break off several pieces of a beignet and toss it at the base of the pole. To my astonishment, he swoops down in a flash, chasing away the pigeons like a seasoned sentry. Though I could find little regarding the symbolism of crows in any of the books loaned to me, I can't shake the feeling that his sudden appearance is more than a coincidence.

Glancing at my watch, I realize time has slipped away once again. I cannot afford to be late for my meeting with Madam Claire. Placing a generous tip beneath my empty cup, I stand to leave, drawing odd looks from fellow patrons as I announce to the bird, "It's time to go!"

On my walk to the park, a mix of curiosity and anxiety bubbles within me. Our meeting today has me on edge. Madam Claire spoke with a sense of urgency the last time we met, but there remained an undercurrent in her voice, something unspoken. It sounded heavy with emotion. With someone like her, who seems to dance between the worlds of the living and the ethereal, you can never be quite sure what lies beneath the surface.

This afternoon the clouds cast a soft, muted light over the park's blooms and greenery, a much-needed reprieve from the oppressive summer humidity. I wander down one of the winding paths, nervous anticipation knotting in my stomach. Finally, I locate the bench beneath the statue of Henry Clay, the meeting spot she chose for our rendezvous. I cannot help but wonder why she picked this statue, given that Clay was more a symbol of Kentucky than Louisiana.

Suddenly, a voice from behind startles me, and my heart leaps into my throat.

"All will be explained, my dear boy."

I spin around, a mix of annoyance and relief washing over me. "I wish you wouldn't do that! My heart literally skipped a beat!"

"Pardon me," she says, her hand gently resting on my shoulder.

"I didn't mean to scare yuh, but I could hear yuh worrin' in dat overactive mind of yours, so I jus' thought I would try to ease yuh concerns. I try not to hear what yuh thinkin' but when it's dat loud, well, Madam Clair can't ignore it."

"Madam Claire," I begin, my voice trembling with a mix of intrigue and apprehension.

"While I'm eager to learn what you have to tell me, I can't shake this feeling of dread. You hold answers to questions that have haunted me for decades, yet I fear it may be best if some were left buried."

"Yuh know, young'un, yuh wise beyond yo years, but don't be too quick to bury what needs to be known. If only yo uncle had been as wise as yuh… maybe we wouldn't be sittin' here today."

I try to maintain my composure, but frustration will not allow it. "There you go again, with those cryptic responses that make no sense!"

"Patience, child. All will come in time. But first, take a breath... clear that spirit of yo's."

Agitated but compliant, I inhale deeply, knowing defiance would only be seen as disrespect. As I exhale, I point to the black crow now perched on the cypress tree providing us with shade.

"My first question, Madam Claire is, why does this bird follow me everywhere? He trailed me home after our first meeting, and I found nothing about crows in any of the books you provided."

"I didn't include dem, mon cher. Dat don't matter none for what we're talkin' 'bout today," she replies, her voice softening as her steely gray eyes bore into mine. "But as for dat bird? He's a messenger, a protector from da spirit world... sent to guide yuh, to keep yuh safe."

"But I don't believe in that stuff, Madam Claire! Or at least I didn't, until all these strange occurrences started piling up." I take a deep breath, steadying my nerves. "Something, or someone, wrecked my room at the boarding house the other day, just like you had warned. And now this crow? All I want is the truth about my uncle and why he deserted our family."

She places her hand over mine, sincerity etched in her features.

"An' yuh will get those answers child. But before we go deeper, I gotta ask yuh somethin'. Did dem books teach yuh anythin'? Not jus' 'bout our religion, but how dis city, dis land, an' da spirits became as one, allowin' our New Orleans voodoo to be more powerful than any other in da world? Yuh gotta learn to see it as more den jus' magic... it's a way of life."

"Madam Claire," I stammer, struggling to sound composed.

"The other day, I thought your voodoo shop was nothing more than a tourist trap, and your theatrical performances were carefully scripted to draw in the crowds. Your stories were entertaining, sure, but that day I viewed them through a skeptical lens. While I have learned much from the books you have given me, I still can't say I believe in all the magic and incantations that go along with what you call your religion, however, I do grasp the spiritual and ritualistic significance behind it all."

"Well, dat's a start, dear. But yuh gotta understand, we are genuine. We ain't pretendin' or actin' for da public. Yuh understand?" She pauses, a knowing look crossing her face. "Yuh ain't curious how I could hear yuh thoughts before yuh saw me?" She asks.

"I figured it was a parlor trick you've mastered over the years."

"No child, our connection, it runs deeper den dat. Deir's an almost kinship between us, one neither of us asked for, but one dat's dare nonetheless. Da story of yo' uncle? Dat ain't for da faint-hearted. We ain't gonna dig into dat jus' yet. But I'll tell yuh dis much, without yuh, yo uncle will never find peace. We gotta forgive each other, an' clear our hearts, before we move forward. An' I gotta tell ya… I hate to admit it but I'm partially responsible for what happened to him."

Anger wells up inside me. *Is she saying that she has known all along what happened to Uncle Ray while I wasted my time studying those damn books?* I leap to my feet, raising my voice.

"Wait, you mean to tell me you've known what happened to my uncle this whole time?!" Suddenly, like an old grainy 8mm reel flickering in my mind, her image and words from the first time we met replay in my mind.

I see myself back in her shop that day.

"I know who yuh are, young man, an' I know why yuh here. Yuh wish to uncover many things, but most important, yuh seek someone."

I sink back onto the bench beside the old woman, who now has a tear glistening in her eye. Taking her hand gently, I speak with newfound resolve.

"I am sorry for my outburst. I just remembered that you tried to tell me from the very start. You knew I was searching for answers about my uncle. I let my emotions take over just now, please forgive me. It's been an exhausting week for me. Madam Claire, what do you need from me today?"

"Did yuh wonder why I chose dis statue, dear?"

"The question had crossed my mind, yes."

"Well, he was known as da Great Compromiser. An' we are here today to do jus' dat, compromise. Yuh say yuh don't believe in magic, but yuh respect our religion child. I would rather yuh accept all aspects of our faith, da religious an' ceremonial, but I will compromise an' share with yuh what I know because I trusts yuh now an' don't think ya'll be doin' anythin' to disrespect us. I need yuh to accept da truth. I know what happened to yo uncle, but I didn't learn da full story 'til jus' last year when my daughter opened up to me right before she passed away."

Madam Claire sits quietly for a few moments as she wipes a tear from her eye.

"Da police couldn't find yo uncle, but he never left dis city, an' he is here. No one, includin' me, knows where though. Dat is what we must find out, yuh an' me. I want yuh to go to da cops an' ask for his files. Yuh might be surprised by what yuh find. Dey got somethin' of his we need to help him rest. It's da only thing linkin' our families together, an' when yuh see it, yuh will know. I can't tell yuh what it is, as it is somethin' yuh muss recognize yuhself, an' understand its value. It will speak to yuh, an' yuh muss' bring it with yuh to our next meetin'. Trust yo instinct, trust da spirit who guides yuh to find it."

"I mean no disrespect Madam Claire, but I am searching for answers, and you promised me you'd tell me everything about my uncle today!"

"Yuh ain't ready yet, cher. When yuh truly believe, when we got dat last piece of da puzzle, den we can put all dis to rest an' give yo uncle da peace he deserves."

I rise from the bench, extending my hand to help her up, but she declines my assistance, reaching for her cane instead.

Before she turns to leave, she adds,

"Once yuh are done wit da police, go back to yo room. Tonight, it's important yuh study yo uncle's journal an' dat little notepad yuh found. We'll meet at my house tomorrow at 10 pm, an' don't be late."

The crow caws loudly and I look over at the branch where it had been perching earlier. He is gone, and looking back to ask one last question, directed at Madam Claire, things get weird.

"But how do you know about the notepad?" I ask of a shadow that is no longer there.

Madam Claire is gone.

Instead, there on the back of the bench where she had been, sits the pet I never wanted, staring at me with his black eyes. "Where did she go?" I ask, as if he could answer.

My question moot, I turn to leave the park.

"She done gone," he says, and I just about jump out of my skin.

"Y…You can talk?" He does not answer the question, just caws like all crows do.

I am just hearing things, I convince myself.

As I leave the park, my faithful companion soars ahead, as if to guide the way.

I stop off at the police station as Madam Claire suggested. The clerk is not too helpful, but after I show her my press credentials, she refers me to a more accommodating officer who knows more about Uncle Ray's case.

The officer greets me with a sturdy handshake. "Mr. Schmitt is it?" he asks.

"I am Officer Deveraux," he says with a smile. "All of us here at the department are disappointed that Mr. Lybarger's case has gone cold for so many years now. Occasionally we reopen old files, but we never seem to discover anything new on the case."

"I understand," I say with a heavy sigh.

"Look, officer," my voice unable to hide my impatience, "I have more than just a journalistic interest in this case. The missing man is my uncle on my mother's side. As his nephew, I may recognize something you have in your reports that may help with this case. There could be something the average detective may have missed. All I am asking is for a chance to look at the reports you have and the interviews you collected to see if there might be a clue or two that has been overlooked."

I do not want to believe the New Orleans Police Department to be incompetent, but I cannot help but think if My uncle were more than just a tourist, if he was indeed a well-known figure in the city, his case may have garnered more attention.

Leading me to a small room he asks me to sit, saying he will return shortly with what files they have on the case. Ten minutes later he enters carrying one file and a box marked Lybarger, 1991.

He sets the box down on the table in front of me shaking his head. "I do not understand why we have this container; it was supposed to be sent to his next of kin many years ago. According to our files, two were sent back to Cincinnati, Ohio to Mrs. Margret Schmitt. You can take that with you once I clear it with the Chief. Of course, the reports stay here."

Before exiting he instructs me to take the file folders back to the clerk's window once I am done and then turns to me one last time and in a solemn voice wishes me luck.

Looking through the materials, my disappointment grows as I realize the officer was correct; their lack of substantial evidence is disheartening. The interviews they conducted during the investigation, if you want to call it that, produced no evidence or leads of any kind. The last page in the file records that the New Orleans police department will close the case and return the three boxes of Uncle Ray's belongings to his sister. I comb through the box and find Uncle Ray's pocketknife and crucifix with the chain broken. Digging deeper I find a small glass vial containing a lock of hair. The extensive reading I have done the past several days has given me the insight to understand the significance of this item. Saphron was sweet on my uncle and wanted to give him a lock of hair so that a part of her would always be with him. Madam Claire said a spirit would speak to me when I found the one thing that binds our families together. I cannot say that happened, but the moment I picked the glass tube up, a warm sensation came over me. I am certain this is what Madam Claire was referring to, so I carefully place it in my pocket.

Once I have thoroughly examined the reports, I gather them together and deliver them to the clerk's window. I watch as she enters the files "returned," and without looking up she announces that I have been given permission to take the box of my uncle's personal belongings with me. I thank her for her time and wish her a good day. Just before leaving the precinct, I see the officer who was so helpful and thank him for his time, letting him know I too, was unable to find anything new.

Exiting the precinct doors carrying what remains of my uncle's life, I contemplate flagging down a cab. I see my new friend and guardian crow patiently waiting outside sitting on the light bar of one of the cruisers parked in front of the precinct. I tell him I am going to take a cab back to the boarding house and will meet him there. Still unaccustomed to my new pet and the fact he can talk, I am again taken aback when he says "no."

"No?" I ask.

"Nice day, walk."

Surely, I cannot allow a bird to dictate how I get home, but then I remember Madam Claire saying that he was sent to watch over me. Perhaps he senses something I cannot, or maybe he just wants company. Whatever it may be, I relent and follow him home awkwardly carrying the box in my arms.

Uncle Ray's Last Request

My winged guide leads me down a much quicker path to the boarding house, and we arrive ten minutes earlier than if I had followed my previous route. I think to myself, *So that's what they mean by "as the crow flies."* This afternoon, I am in too much of a hurry to indulge in pleasantries with the staff and residents of the boarding house. I dash upstairs to do as Madam Claire suggested, comb through Uncle Ray's journal and the small notepad I found last night. Just the fact that she knew about the hidden pad from so many years ago both confuses and amazes me. There is more to her religion than I thought possible. I must accept that it provides her with powers I will never understand. No matter how hard I try, I will never get used to her being able to enter my thoughts.

I have read Uncle Ray's journal more times than I can count but always skip the parts that seemed unrelated to his disappearance or would be of no help in my article. But this time, my fingers pause on the second-to-last page. There is something strange there; a cryptic message, written as if it is more of a code than a phrase. "Remember, it is not a poem." I read on but find nothing to elaborate on this strange passage, other than song lyrics written in green ink.

I turn my attention to the unexpected discovery, the weathered old pad I halfheartedly leafed through yesterday. His nearly illegible handwriting and scribbles show signs of a disorganized and perhaps, dare I say, mentally ill man. His words run into each other and stray marks scatter across the pages. Uncle Ray's thoughts seem disjointed and even chaotic in certain areas. One name keeps cropping up, Celeste. Beyond that, I can find no new or helpful information. Frustrated, I toss the notepad aside. It lands on top of Uncle Ray's journal, the gray back of the pad face-up. And that is when I see it, the same phrase I first read in his journal. "Remember, it's not a poem." I sit back. What could that mean? Eagerly, I grab his journal and flip through the thin sheets of paper, back to the second-to last-page, and read what I thought were song lyrics written in green. My stomach tightens. Why had I not seen this before? In no way would these words ever find themselves in a song.

To find me now, say this phrase.
Then you will see my final days.
Trust your heart to the words I share.
And I will gladly take you there.
My heart skips. What the hell is this? The words feel like an invitation, strangely enticing, but something feels off, and it brings a shiver to my soul. The phrase feels … wrong, and not just grammatically. He has created a sense of unease by the peculiar word choice and arrangement. I sort through the books Madam

Claire loaned me and find the one titled Spells and Incantations for Beginners. I quickly turn the pages, my heart racing. I locate the chapter listed as "*Spells for the Young and Inexperienced.*"

"Well, if that isn't just what I am looking for," I snort. I land on page 285, my fingers trembling as I read: "A successful incantation begins with honoring the spirits."

Light a candle in reverence.

Have a personal item in your presence.

Say the words,

But mean them true,

And success shall follow you.

But beware: the misuse of spells and charms,

Can also lead to great harm.

What is with the rhyming? I ask myself. *It is a little over the top don't you think?"* I mean, yeah, I have watched many movies and all spell seem to rhyme, but is that even a spell? I hardly think it is, it reads like a warning in poem form.

The Chapter continues to list several generic spells for the inexperienced to practice. As I read on, it also insists that none of these spells, incantations, or prayers are to be attempted without an experienced practitioner supervising.

I need not worry. With no candle or Madam Claire to guide me, it seems risky to even contemplate acting on the thoughts running through my mind. Something tells me that if I do attempt to follow through, it may be the worst decision I ever make. I shove the book aside, deciding to spend no more energy on such ideas.

As the clock strikes 2 pm, I realize I need to replenish my groceries. Before shopping I opt for a nice warm bowl of gumbo at a nearby eatery. If nothing else, that should help settle my nervous stomach. After my late lunch, I walk to the drugstore in the Quarter and a thought gnaws at me. Where's my crow? I have not seen him since this morning. I then realize his disappearance bothers me more than I care to admit.

Collecting the items needed and a few impulse purchases as well, I take my spot at the end of the long line waiting to check out. Once it is my turn, I prepare to hand over my credit card to the clerk. Then I hear the unmistakable sound of flapping wings. Taking advantage of an incoming customer, my shadow finds his way into the store. *There he is*, I say to myself, *my albatross*. He lands on a candle in a tall glass container, with The Holy Mother Mary depicted in glitter, on the front label. His beady eyes lock onto mine as if to say, "You didn't wait for me." The clerk glares at him. "Shoo!" she snaps. But the crow refuses to move.

She crumples up a piece of paper and throws it in his direction. Not even coming close to hitting the bird, I decide to step in and deescalate the situation. "I'll get him," I say, trying to calm the clerk as she scowls.

"Mister, those are disease-ridden birds, worse than pigeons."

The crow caws loudly, seemingly in protest to her snide remark, causing her to shriek.

I walk over to the shelf where the candle is displayed and whisper, "You got to leave." While customers watch in awe, I open the door and the bird flies out. To make things right, I pick up the candle and pay for it, apologizing for the disturbance the bird caused.

Exiting the store, I look up at my latest dependent and mutter under my breath,

"You cost me three bucks, you flying rodent."

Shaking my head, I add, "Come on, let's head out."

Once again, he leads me through the Quarter, gliding through the air as if he knows secrets about this place I'll never understand. Back in my room, I unpack the groceries, placing some trail mix and bread on a plate as I open the window, finally accepting I have a new feathered companion and therefore must make certain he is fed.

I lie on the bed and try to unwind, but my new unwanted shadow becomes a persistent nuisance. He is completely disinterested in the food and water I prepared, leaving them untouched. Pecking repeatedly on the window, I let the crow in so as not to rile any of the other guests here. I place my finger on my lips whispering, "you must remain quiet, or I will put you right back outside." I lay back down hoping to get some much-needed rest.

Landing on the desk the bird immediately focuses on the candle. Pecking at it, first gently, then harder as his frustration seems to grow. "What do you want?" I ask. He ignores me, pecking even harder, his beak making sharp sounds against the glass. Then, suddenly, he hops to the old journal, pulling it next to the candle with an urgency that truly confuses me. "What do you want?" I repeat. I get out of bed and sit down at the small desk hoping to calm the bird.

The obsessed crow looks first at me and then at the journal. He does this several times, eventually pecking at the candle again. "Got a match?" he asks. His request is now quite clear. Remaining apprehensive, I finally give in to his demands. After all, according to Madam Claire, he is not only my guardian but also a messenger sent from the spirit world.

There was a reason for him landing on the candle, there seems to be a reason for everything he does. What I have learned these past few days is that none of what is happening is coincidental. My first meeting with Madam Claire in her shop, him following me home, and the feelings and sudden unexplained intuition I have been experiencing. They all seem related, as if to guide me towards the answers I seek.

"Okay, okay…" I mutter, my voice shaking. "But I don't want to do this. I'm afraid." He hops onto my shoulder, pressing his small head against my cheek, as if to reassure me that what it is he is asking me to do will bring me no harm.

The sensation is strange, yet somehow comforting. With his message delivered, the crow lets out a low caw and flies to the window pecking at the glass again. I open it, allowing him to leave and enjoy the evening air. I shake my head still in disbelief as I watch my new friend finally eat the food I plated for him earlier.

Sitting back down at the desk, I take a deep breath, filled with uncertainty. *Do you really want to do this?* I ask myself. The words in green ink seem to promise answers, and it is all too tempting.

My hand trembles in fear as I strike the red tipped match on the side of the small cardboard container. Using my other hand to steady the flame, I light the candle. With great trepidation, I turn to the page in Uncle Ray's journal that has the words I once thought to be song lyrics.

In an uncertain and shaky voice, I speak the words: "To find me now, say this phrase. Then you will see my final days. Trust your heart to the words I share. And I will gladly take you there." I do not know what I was expecting but reciting the words accomplished nothing. I chuckle and shake my head. My doubts are confirmed. Wanting to prove to myself this was all superstition, I recite the words once again, more clearly, more firmly. Still nothing.

Suddenly a noise from under the bed grabs my attention. It sounded like a book falling to the floor. The words *Coincidence or a poltergeist* echo clearly in my mind. I check under the bed and find the book titled Spells and Incantations for Beginners, not only on the floor, but opened to page 285. Then I remember there is something in there regarding the casting of spells.

If what is written in green ink is indeed a spell or prayer, this book provides the instructions I need to complete this task.

I cautiously slide the book from under the bed as I read again the passage pertaining to spells and incantations.

A successful incantation begins with honoring the spirits.
Light a candle in reverence
Have a personal item in your presence.
Say the words, but mean them true.
And success shall follow you.

I need a personal item, something that once belonged to Uncle Ray. Looking around, the choice is obvious. His favorite hat will allow me to establish a greater and more personal connection to him. I wrap my hands around the frayed brim, the texture familiar and comforting, and repeat the phrase once again. I close my eyes and whisper the words from my heart.

"To find me now, say this phrase. Then you will see my final days. Trust your heart to the words I share, and I will gladly take you there." And then, everything goes dark.

Walking a Mile in His Shoes

My choice to recite the words I found in Uncle Ray's journal has immediate consequences. The room spins, and at that moment, everything descends into murky darkness. Time slows, stretching into an unbearable stillness. As I slowly open my eyes, I am surrounded by a hazy, eerie glow. My body, no, my essence, hovers weightlessly in nothingness as I try to focus. I am here, but not here. Blurred colors grow sharper and muffled sounds turn into festive music and laughter that swirl freely as the streets come to life. I watch, no, *feel,* the rhythm and pulse of the Mardi Gras celebration as it plays out below me. But then, the voices and music start to fade. Slowly, the crowd and noises dissipate. Not wanting to leave, I desperately reach out, but my soul is being torn away from the revelers by an invisible rope. No longer anchored, I watch helplessly as it all vanishes into a faint echo. This moment feels like a memory, yet strangely unfamiliar.

I feel my soul pulled backward, spiraling toward the boarding house. But even here, I am no longer physically present. The room is familiar, yet wrong. The walls and furniture seem altered, as if time and space itself have become a warped reflection of how things were just moments ago.

A sickly sense of detachment overtakes me. Reminiscent of the day I rented the room, this feels much stronger and much more deliberate. My spirit struggles to hold on. It is like I am living someone else's life, seeing the world through their eyes and feeling emotions that are not my own. I can only compare this sensation to viewing a movie or perhaps finding yourself in the middle of a terrible dream.

I watch while strange hands in front of me perform a particularly mundane task. Meticulously they hang and straighten clothes that are not my own in the same armoire I placed my wardrobe in just a few days ago. However, this time a nice cedar scent escapes the cabinet instead of the pungent odor of mothballs I smelled the first time I threw its doors open. The paint is brighter and not peeling on the small chest of drawers, and oddly enough sitting on the nightstand is the lamp which had been broken by a malevolent spirit only a few days ago. The room itself looks freshly remodeled.

A strange consciousness takes hold of me. It is the feeling of accomplishment. *Why? I haven't done anything.* It is now that I realize this individual's emotions are flowing through me as well. These unnerving perceptions or vibes are overwhelming, yet familiar, like a distant memory I cannot quite place. There is comfort, but also a deep undercurrent of wrongness. It feels like I am wearing someone else's skin.

I have no control over what is happening and am merely a passenger along for the ride, unable to halt the actions as they play out before me. I become dizzy as the room abruptly spins while my host's feet step away from the armoire. I can hear the chair being pulled away from the desk but cannot see the action taking place. I watch as hands, older than my own, hover over an old typewriter. Fingers fly over the letters with precision, the rhythmic click-clack of keys striking the sheet of paper fills the silence of the room. I watch as words appear before me:

"New Orleans, known as the Crescent City..."

I can feel the sensation and reaction of the keys. I am writing, but the words are not my own. My eyes trace each letter as they materialize on the page, forming sentences that seem to have a life of their own. I read the narrative as it appears before me, but these are not my words or vocabulary.

"This city holds hidden treasures and a mystique quite rare," the typewriter sings.

"Here there is a culture steeped in mystery and untold secrets. You can hear it whispered about in dark alleyways or hushed conversations being held in dimly lit jazz clubs..."
The hands stop briefly as if the writer is lost in thought.

"There's a deeper truth beneath the surface of this tourist's destination, something unsettling. I may have uncovered an undercurrent of New Orleans, which most are unaware of. What I have stumbled upon is a part of this city's history and culture very few people speak about in everyday conversation."
I sense a tightness in the chest, but not my own. The person typing has become beset by emotion.

"Saphron promises to teach me more about this hidden world. She calls it voodoo, says it's her religion. Outsiders, especially those of my skin tone, are discouraged from learning or knowing about it, but I didn't care. When I first became aware of this strange culture, I brushed it off as superstitious nonsense made up by the locals to take money from gullible tourists. But Saphron, she has shown me things I can't explain. As a token of her affection, she gifted me an amulet, explaining it was prayed over by a high priestess. She says it will bring me luck. Recent

events have proven her right. However, it is important, she warns, to understand that the gift can produce positive   , or very unfortunate results, depending on the person and their disposition. I wish I had paid more attention to those words sooner."

The keys continue to clack under my fingers, sharp and insistent, typing words I am not thinking, but somehow, instinctively know are about to be written.

"Nothing in this city is as it seems," I watch the keys type. Even before the line is complete, a chill settles over me. *"Saphron tried to warn me. She said this city's secrets could steal a man's soul if he was not careful."*

The lines pour from me, with an odd rhythm I am helpless to stop. These hands are driven by memories older than I, writing words that reek of regret and something darker. I sense a distant shiver.

And suddenly, silence. The keys discontinue their repetitious cadence.

It may already be too late.

I hear, but it is not my thought, this one belongs to my uncle.

Air fills my lungs with a breath I did not take. I feel the body rise from the chair and then a stark realization hits. With the words in front of me, I do not want to admit to myself this is happening. Any remaining doubt is removed, as the eyes I am looking through are not my own. The same mirror I have used for days, yet much newer, reveals my suspicion to be correct. How can this be? How can he be here?

I sense an uncontrollable urge to leave this room. *Where does he want to go?* I watch as his hand reaches for a hat nearby. I can feel his fingers trace along the brim, the nails faintly yellowed and unfamiliar, as they lift the hat to my head. Suddenly, the mirror reveals what my boggled mind refuses to grasp. It is not me adjusting that fedora to just the right angle. The gesture feels practiced and automatic, as though these hands have performed this action thousands of times before. But it cannot be me, I hate wearing hats. I feel the wool press against the crown of his head, its warmth unfamiliar, almost alien, and yet a sense of pride accompanied by a smirk falls across his face beneath the fedora.

I am not just watching his actions; I am living his life with him, hearing his thoughts as my own. His emotions, desires, and fears flow through me like an unstoppable current.

Somehow, through some twist of fate, his memories and consciousness have bled into mine, weaving a parallel thread between our lives. Together, we are living these moments. The incantation must have triggered some deep connection we share across time and space. His life, his past, now a vivid thread woven into my present.

I stand here, staring at the reflection, and for a moment, no longer is there a division between us. His life and his choices have become mine as well.

I cannot say for certain what is happening, but the more I become part of his existence, the thinner the line between our realities becomes. What began as a disorienting nightmare is now something far more real and inescapable. I am now walking in Uncle Ray's shoes, carrying the weight of his decisions, choices, and secrets.

As I accept these facts, a deep sense of foreboding closes in around me, and I grow frightened. I have no control over what is happening. What if he gets into trouble? If this is when he comes up missing will I return to the present? Will my essence be lost here forever? My emotions and fear run rampant, and I am helpless to stop them. I can only watch as the world in which he lives passes before my eyes.

It is then a question begins to gnaw at me: Is it him living through me or, am I living through him?

Madam Celeste

A disjointed feeling floods over me, more unsettling than anything I have ever known. He is going somewhere and thinks he is looking fabulous. To me, his Columbo-style trench coat and fedora are far too much; it is overkill. I have always hated hats, and this monstrosity does nothing to persuade me otherwise. *Why did Uncle Ray think it suited him and just where exactly does he think he's going?* I remind myself that the incantation from his journal is supposed to help me understand his last days, not to harm me, but still...it is unnerving, watching him like a character in a movie. *Just sit back, watch and learn,* I tell myself.

Outside the boarding house the wind howls as a chill fills the air. My uncle shivers, and though I have no skin I feel it as well. He walks to a small car and as he unlocks the door, a wave of stale cigarette smoke rolls out, making me recoil instinctively. I have no breath to hold but wish I did. What a revolting smell. He adjusts the mirror, fastens his seat belt, and reaches into the armrest for a fresh pack of cigarettes. "Geez no, Uncle Ray!" I yell, knowing he cannot hear. He lights one and the warmth of the smoke fills his lungs. My stomach churns with disgust; I long to snatch it away but am utterly powerless to stop him. He exhales an annoying cloud of smoke, cracking the driver's window as Bryan Adams blares through the speakers: "Everything I do, I do it for you." Oh, Uncle Ray, your taste in music and vices leave a lot to be desired.

I can only watch as he weaves through New Orleans' French Quarter, honking at drunks who stagger into the road. "Get outta the way, damn drunks!" he shouts, laughing, as some fling their middle fingers in response. After circling several blocks in search of a free space, he finally finds one, and struggles to parallel park, mumbling curses under his breath. With a final satisfied sigh, he straightens his hat and walks towards one of the many bars on this street, whistling as if he does not have a care in the world. *Seriously, Uncle Ray, a drinker and smoker? What's next, a joint in the bathroom?*

Pushing the double swinging doors open, a cloud of secondhand smoke escapes the club as music plays softly. Jazz has never been a preferred genre of mine, but obviously they know Uncle Ray by name at this bar, as they already have a beer waiting for him.

As he attempts to pay for his drink, the bartender pushes his hand away.

"Heard about the young girl you been seeing. Sorry for your loss."

Young girl? Loss? This is news to me. Uncle Ray tips his hat and in a mournful voice answers, "She was a special lady. It's a real tragedy. She told me of her heart condition but swore her medication kept it in check."

Before walking away from the bar, he leaves the previously rejected five-dollar bill as a tip. "Thanks for the beer, man."

He wanders to a table in the corner, nursing his beer as he pulls out his journal from his jacket, clicking his pen before writing. He scrawls a name across the page: *Saphron.* I do not remember seeing any mention of the death of a young woman in the journal I have been reading. Words flow from his pen as I watch his hand move with lyrical ease, each line pulling me in deeper.

I met her in a voodoo shop on Royal Street. Like most old souls, she was young but had an aura about her, as though she'd lived many lifetimes. There was more to her than I could ever fathom. She ran the shop one night a week for her grandmother and was the one responsible for making the shop's strange trinkets and burlap voodoo dolls that felt almost alive. I am very uncomfortable with all this nonsense, but realize dark magic is part of New Orleans and writing about it may spice up my article.

I feel Uncle Ray's face relax as he takes a sip of beer and continues to write, reliving a sweet and special moment.

She looked into my eyes, breaking through all my discomfort, her gaze warm and inviting. I remember her first words, "Where are you from, dear? *She asked with a bright smile.* "Nothing here should frighten you. It's not what you think. To earn a living, some of us play along with the public's misconception of our religion."

With those words, she had captivated my interest. Where most people who come into places like these are tourists looking for souvenirs, magical candles, or potions, I view visiting the shop and this experience through my reporter's eye, seeing this as potential data for a very exciting and informative article.

Looking away from his writing, he takes another sip of beer. Finding it warm now, he nearly spits it out. The taste is disgusting and makes my stomach churn. As a mere spectator, I am grateful, or it would have made me gag. Along with him, I feel a maintained sense of grief and remorse as he makes his way back to the bar. A jolt of electricity shocks both of us as a hand reaches out and touches his. He stops and looks down at a colorfully dressed woman wearing an olive-green turban. Despite not necessarily fitting in, she appears to be a fixture. A chill grips us both, freezing him mid-step, and for a moment, her gaze lands squarely on me, or rather, through me. I feel exposed. Is it possible she can see us both? As she stares deep into Uncle Ray's eyes and mine, I feel my soul shiver.

Still unnerved by the odd woman, Ray saunters back to his table with a beer in hand, unable to shake the strange encounter. Trying to focus on his journal, his pen pauses every now and again as his gaze drifts back to the strange woman in the green headdress. Finally, he scribbles the last lines of Saphron's story.

Before I had to end things with her, she gave me a gift I will always hold dear, a small glass vial with a lock of her hair. She claimed it to be a token of her affection that would bind our souls together always, insisting we would remain connected to one another no matter where life took us. This was too much, I had taken advantage of her emotions, and I let the situation become too serious. To spare her any more pain I would have to end our friendship. The night I broke it off between us, she became extremely angry, crying while in the same breath cursing at me in Creole.

The thought of hurting her filled me with a sickening dread. She forced a decision upon me, and I would have to admit that unfortunately I could never reciprocate her affections. This is not the first time something like this has happened. In the past, I have used the line, "I have a fiancé," to discourage ladies from becoming too attached. It was the excuse I used to cover up the real reason I could not be in a serious relationship. It always worked, though I would have to endure the wrath of a scorned woman for several weeks after speaking that lie to them. I was prepared for the same reaction when I used the lie on Saphron. Wiser than her years, the young woman did not fall for the fake fiancé line, and I would be forced to admit the truth about myself. I didn't know she'd get sick, let alone pass away. Had I, perhaps I would not have revealed my secret to her. She refused to believe me, exclaiming that I did not look or act "that way." I thought sharing the truth about myself would help her better understand why I had to end our friendship. Maybe if she were older my honesty would not have affected her as profoundly. Perhaps she would still be alive had I continued the charade. After all, I was a visitor here and lived so far away, the chances of us ever seeing

I do not remember reading one word of this story in his journal. Could it be he kept more than one? My question becomes moot once I watch him tear the pages from the binder. I can feel his love and reverence for her as he folds them and places the pages tenderly in the inside pocket of his coat.

His grief is palpable and mingles with mine. We are both jarred as from behind him a hand touches his shoulder, and the chill I felt earlier surges back. He turns around to see the woman in the turban, her stare, sharp as a knife. She leans in close and whispers, "Bring to me a red wine, dear boy. I believe we have much to discuss."

Along with him I can feel a pull at his consciousness. The urge to obey her request is undeniable. It feels like there is an invisible yet physical force pushing us forward. As we grow close to the bar, I see a beer and a red wine already waiting for us.

"I be taking it you are getting this for Madam Celeste?" The bartender asks.

"Yes," Uncle Ray answers, "and I have no idea why."

"Oh, it is best you don't worry 'bout that. Consider it an honor, she chose and trusts you.

The bartender's cryptic response has both Ray and I intrigued. Through his eyes, I watch as he sets the drinks down, respectfully asking if he may join her. She tilts her head ever so slightly, and I feel a strange pull, as though this power she has over him extends to me as well, fusing the three of us together.

This event leads to Uncle Ray finding himself completely bound by Madam Celeste, voodoo, and the colorful history of New Orleans.

Coming Out of the Trance

The last thing I remember is Uncle Ray setting two drinks down on the worn tabletop. A mellow saxophone solo, interwoven with brushed drums, filled the air as his eyes remained fixed on this strikingly beautiful, yet unfamiliar woman. Her presence is mesmerizing and exotic. With features as if sculpted by the hands of Michelangelo himself, each curve and line of her face is a masterpiece of genetic design. I can sense how very taken he is with her. Though I cannot see it, I feel a broad smile overtaking his face as he stands there and for a moment loses his breath. Curious as to what she wants to talk about, he asks to join her. I, however, perceive something quite different within her, and fear courses through me. I want to yell out, run Uncle Ray, run!

Why does he stay? Can he not sense the power she has over him? Does he not see the sinister look in her eyes? Why is he not recognizing these red flags?

She has a commanding presence, both mysterious and alluring. He seems oblivious to the power she holds over him, but I, as a mere spectator, can sense his inability to resist. Something dark and intriguing is drawing him in. There is a dangerous and forbidden aura about her. I begin to feel him try to resist, but it is too late, his efforts are futile. She does not answer his request, there is no need. I can hear her voice in his head say, "Please have a seat," as we both feel him slowly pull out the chair across from her. I suddenly begin to feel dizzy and disoriented as if I am losing my grip on reality.

I cannot fight what is happening. The familiar vortex like power I felt earlier when all this began, begins to pull my soul backward.

I close my eyes to the unsettling and ghostly visions. When I reopen them, my sight is once again blurred, like watching fog dissipate as it lifts gently from the streets. Every object in the room slowly sharpens. My laptop's fan hums quietly on the desk, having replaced the antiquated typewriter I saw mere moments ago. I rise and walk over to the wardrobe, swinging the doors open. I am once again greeted with the pungent odor of mothballs instead of the fresh cedar smell from before. Mine are now the clothes hanging inside. It takes several minutes before I come back to my senses and understand that what I just endured is over, and that I am back where it all started. But was it real? Did it genuinely happen? The abhorrent taste of burnt cigarettes in my mouth is one I wish never to experience again, and that is all the evidence I need to convince myself this was no hallucination.

I shudder, running my hand over my face. What the hell was that? A dream? No dream has ever felt this real. I may never fully grasp the unsettling events that transpired, but I know with absolute certainty that I will never again utter that incantation, nor any other.

An overpowering and lingering unease clings to me as I try to come to terms with the things I witnessed. Whether any of it truly happened, what occurred felt real enough and will serve as a chilling reminder to me that some things are best left undisturbed.

I thumb through Uncle Ray's journal, searching for answers. Who was that woman? Perhaps that meeting, if it occurred at all, came from a hidden corner of Uncle Ray's memory, shrouded in shadows and secrets. Is it possible this was a clandestine event he never meant to share with anyone, including me?

Why I am Here

Though it felt like I spent an entire day with the man I never got to know, I look over at the alarm clock and am shocked to see less than thirty minutes have passed. Now completely disoriented, I try to put the horribly uncomfortable experience behind me. I must focus on why I am here in New Orleans. Like my uncle, I have allowed myself to become distracted from my purpose for this visit. I still have an article to write and must get back on schedule. Serendipitously, the laptop pings softly, reminding me it waits patiently for my attention and is more than ready to begin the assignment.

Thrusting my arms forward to push my sleeves up, I open a blank document. I close my eyes tightly, searching my brain for a tentative title. And it comes to me.

"Be Warned: New Orleans Can Captivate and Steal Your Soul."

The words, however, stop there. I stare at the blinding white page. The cursor flashes sarcastically, mocking me as I sit here unable to expound on the title. I realize that despite several days here, my understanding of New Orleans remains confined to brochures, tourist traps and my brief foray into the French Quarter. Without first getting to know this city, how can I craft an interesting narrative that authentically portrays New Orleans's unique blend of culinary delights, compelling history, and cultural nuances. I will not be able to continue this article until I experience the city whose rich culture and heritage beckons me.

Well, at least I came up with a title, I tell myself as I remove the watch from my pocket. Having booked a walking tour for this evening I must prepare to meet the group at North Rampart at 6:00pm.

After showering, I dress and exit my room making sure to check my wallet before stepping out into the humid evening air. Out of character for me, I leave with Uncle Ray's fedora perched atop my head. Not being used to any kind of head covering, this is an odd yet comforting sensation, that somehow just feels right. Though I do not share his fashion sense, I can accept that it was as much a part of him as my pocket watch is to me.

The streets are alive, humming with music and festive visitors, as though this city itself is alive and breathing. As I arrive in the French Quarter early, I enjoy the ambiance New Orleans provides. The sight of neon signs juxtaposed with the amber glow of the ornate lamp posts which light up the street and the incredible music flowing from the open windows of bars. Inebriated tourists staggering aimlessly and haphazardly discarded food in the streets all make for an image that will remain in my mind for days to come. I watch as carnival-like barkers try to lure and entice naïve young men into their bars with promises of seeing the world's most beautiful and scantily clad women, who, for the right price, will bare it all. The party-like atmosphere is thrilling and inviting. It is easy to see how one can lose themselves in such an atmosphere.

The noise of the revelry tug at me, tempting me to lose myself in the festivities, but I remind myself why I am here.

Tonight is not for indulgence. I am here to learn about a city whose story is waiting to be uncovered. The best way to understand New Orleans is to walk its streets with someone who knows its heart and soul. There are many walking tours to choose from, each offering a slice of the city's complex history and lore, but the voodoo tour interests me the most. Tomorrow, I have booked a separate excursion which will allow me to immerse myself in the historic side of the Crescent City. But this evening I want to learn of the mysteries that lurk beneath the city's vibrant surface.

The guides who narrate the walking tours are more than just storytellers and historians; they are stewards of the past who are passionate about their city in a way that promises to leave tourists and history buffs alike with more than just facts. These treks come with an unspoken promise that those who participate will walk away with a deep and lasting connection to this special city whose past is as alive as its present.

With over-the-top gestures, the guide regales us with epic sagas of the spirit world and how it interacts with citizens and tourists visiting New Orleans. She speaks of spells, incantations, and the saints and Loas who watch over the city. I am more convinced than ever that my uncle embarked on such a venture and became engrossed in the stories shared by the guides, and that it is tales such as these which led him to the voodoo shop where he would meet Saphron.

To completely understand this vibrant city, I must also take a tour based on the recorded past of New Orleans. Tomorrow's pilgrimage will be one based on factual knowledge. I am certain it will prove to be more informative regarding New Orleans' history as a city, instead of the mythical and spiritual side represented during tonight's two-hour presentation. I do find it funny that our guide, as a woman, chose to dress as the Loa known as Baron Samedi. Down to the silk top hat and with her face painted to resemble a skull she indeed resembled the deity, right down to his cane topped with a tiny skull.

After tipping the hard-working lady whose costume was a bit much, I plan to reward myself by joining the partiers I left earlier, however, my stomach has other ideas, notifying me that it is nearing 8pm and time for dinner. I long for something different. I have a craving for old fashioned comfort food. No matter how much I am enjoying the unique dishes offered up in the restaurants and cafés in the French Quarter, lately I have been craving home cooking. I want good old fashioned non-Cajun infused fried chicken with mac and cheese. I overheard someone in the boarding house speak of a restaurant nearby that serves country style cuisine for those who cannot handle or have had enough of the spicy creole dishes for which New Orleans is famous. Tonight, my tongue and stomach will enjoy a break from the exotic and enjoy a fulfilling yet rather bland meal.

Finding Ray's Old Haunt

After dinner I need to walk around for a while and before I know it, I find myself on Carondelet. My feathered companion has been missing this evening and without his guidance I allowed myself to veer off course.

And then I see it. A block away, beckoning for me to come in for a visit. Fate seems to keep drawing me here. The once bright neon sign in the window flickers faintly, *Jazz Note*. Taking a deep breath, I step inside. The old wooden doors creak, announcing my arrival. It looks and feels quite different at this hour. The dim lighting and emptiness causes it to seem less inviting than before.

I surmise this bar must be a late-night destination for locals and tourists, as when I met Madam Claire here the other evening it was far livelier. A weary eyed bartender greets me, his voice low and raspy.

"What'll it be?" he grumbles.

"Just a coke," I answer.

Ordering a nonalcoholic drink seems to upset the bartender and with a disapproving huff, he fills a glass with ice and soda, placing it atop a napkin while refusing to make eye contact.

"One dollar."

I hand him two.

Since it was so late when I met Madam Claire here, I did not focus much on the ambiance of this bar, and it seems like a different place at this hour. This evening however, I take inventory and make a mental note of everything I see. Looking around, it remains exactly as it appeared fifteen years ago, or at least the way Uncle Ray saw it through his eyes. The tables look as if they have recently been refurbished, the old wooden chairs, however, still show their age. Remembering the vision, I retrace my uncle's steps to where he decided to sit that night so many years ago. The same table nearby where the mysterious woman sat, is empty, but I can see her ghostly figure just as she appeared that evening, in her colorful outfit looking beautiful but quite out of place.

Something is very different. The ambiance is way off. Though I appreciate being able to breathe clean air, the smoke that lingered and encapsulated this bar many years ago is no longer, and to be honest, it does not feel much like an old Jazz Club anymore. Replacing the brass trio, piano and stage, is a silent, dust-covered jukebox, now a testament to past performances now lost to time. Wanting to break the silence, I decide to liven up the joint by playing some of my favorite songs. Scanning the list, I notice only Dixieland Jazz and a few ancient country songs. I am in no mood for either. Ice rattles in the bottom of my cocktail glass and I walk back to the bar for a refill and to complain. The bartender sells me the refill but wants to hear none of my grousing.

"Look fella, this used to be a jazz bar many years ago and even though no one plays here anymore, the owners still want to keep the memory alive.”

“I understand, was just trying to liven up the place, but all you have on the jukebox is old jazz and outdated country music.”

“Wearing an old hat like that, I thought you would be a jazz loving man.”

“Nah, it is a family heirloom, and I just felt like giving it one last tour of the Quarter.”

And then the oddest thing occurred. From behind the bar, he brings out a flashlight, shining it directly in my face.

“What the hell man?! Are you trying to blind me?!”

“Naw sir,” he replies, “it’s just that, well…. don’t see too many of those type of hats ‘round anymore and they were never really popular here in New Orleans. Just wanted to get a look at it is all. Sorry, didn’t mean to upset ya, As I said, don’t see too many like that ‘round here and last time I did, well…I don’t want to speak out of turn. Sorry again.”

Not that he deserves an explanation, but since I am bored and to further the conversations, I decide to ease the man’s curiosity.

“It was my uncle’s favorite hat, and a staple of his wardrobe. Last time he wore it, I think it was right here in this bar.”

“Was he a small squirrely kind of dude? I don’t mean no disrespect, but someone who looked like you, but smaller, was a customer here many years ago. A little reporter feller, asked too many questions.”

“What kind of questions?” I press.

“He was curious about local legends. Stories about things better left alone.” The old bartender’s tone grows darker and less friendly now.

“He started poking his nose in places it did not belong. He wanted to know everything about our history and way of life.” He makes a motion for me to draw closer to the bar.

I lean in a little too closely and can tell he has imbibed in a peppermint schnapps shot or two during his shift.

“Look here, there’s a reason New Orleans keeps its secrets from the outside world. But that little feller wouldn’t heed anyone’s advice and well, let’s just say, from what I hear, he paid a steep price for his curiosity and insistence.”

The air between us becomes tense as the conversation strains. I take out a twenty and push it towards him, hoping to loosen his tongue. “I am listening,” I say, but he shakes his head and declines.

Refusing my bribe, he pushes the bill back towards me. “Some stories don’t bear repeating kid. Best let the dead rest.”

I had not planned on coming here tonight and did not expect to discuss my uncle, so I am disappointed when the bartender refuses to share more information. I decide to cut my losses and call it a night. It is getting late, and I need to head back to the boarding house.

Finding Uncle Ray

As the sun peeks through the clouds over New Orleans, I am wrestling with a sense of growing uncertainty regarding my impending meeting with Madam Claire. I leave the boarding house with great trepidation. The past few days have been a myriad of ups and downs. This has become an emotional rollercoaster I wish to no longer ride, but for the sake of closure, I must. On the walk to her home, as it is quite near my residence, there is plenty of time to think, perhaps too much.

A knot of unease tightens within my stomach as I grow closer to the address she has written down. I had not expected such a dramatic difference between my imagined version of her home and the one that is coming into view. The light blue facade, trimmed with vibrant pink gingerbread molding, is almost whimsical, a jarring counterpoint to the reputation associated with the woman who lives within. A cheerful welcome mat lay directly beneath a stern "No Solicitors" sign posted in bold letters just below the doorknocker. The combination of both items feels inviting and foreboding, as though the house itself gets to decide who crosses its threshold.

As the door creaks open, her warm home welcomes me like a soft blanket. Smells of cinnamon spice and the flicker of candles play across the colorfully painted walls adorned with ceremonial masks and hand carved wooden shields. The living room, illuminated by soft golden lamplight, is a surprising contrast to her dark and mystical shop. Nothing in this beautifully decorated house hints that a voodoo priestess lives here. Clearly, when at home, she wishes to distance herself from the label the locals associate with her name. Only the essence of a proud, welcoming woman steeped in tradition and family values resides here. Above the hearth, an ornately carved mantle displays a timeline of her family's lineage, frozen in photographs. Generations watch over her with knowing eyes, as they promise never to reveal her secrets.

Madam Claire crosses in front of me, the hem of her dress brushing against the polished hardwood floor. She gestures towards a loveseat lined with silk covered pillows.

"Make yo'self comfortable," she insists in a voice both rich and calm. "I'll be right back."

I try to find a comfortable position on the overstuffed loveseat but cannot. Still nervous, my eyes won't rest. They take inventory of each piece of art adorning her walls. Milky white busts sit on pedestals around the room with artificial flowered wreaths carefully encircling the base of each one. My vision once again becomes focused on the mantle. Almost calling to me, I rise and approach the photographs, the craftsmanship of the wooden frames too beautiful not to touch. The pictures capture lives long past, vigorous men, regal women, and among them, one face that appears repeatedly. A young girl, vibrant and beautiful. Madam Claire has them displayed in the order in which the young girl aged. First a toddler, then 2 years old, until the final one in full color, showing a young debutante proudly modeling her new formal dress. Like a stop motion film, the pictures capture her moments of joy and innocence until, abruptly, the series ends. It takes a moment, but I make the connection. *Oh god, that's Saphron.* my mind whispers.

"Yuh are right," a sorrowful voice says from behind. Startled, the picture shakes, nearly dropping from my hand.

"Dat is my granddaughter, Saphron."

Madam Claire's presence fills the room like a sudden rush of wind. Her uncanny ability to read thoughts has unnerved me before, but now it leaves my heart beating rapidly in my throat.

She slides gracefully around the coffee table, setting a silver tray down. A steaming teapot and a plate of gingersnap cookies welcome me. "Sit," she instructs, motioning to the loveseat. "We have much to discuss."

I obey as my heart continues to race. The power of her words settle over me, demanding yet somehow comforting, too. She pours the tea and holds the tray of cookies out in a gesture for me to take one. I declined her offer.

"Yuh need yo energy," she insists. "Take one now. Later yuh will be glad yuh did."

As I take a sip of the comforting tea and reluctantly bite into the cookie, she begins her tale in a chilling narrative woven from heartbreak and revenge; one I had also read about in an old journal. My uncle, the man I had come here seeking answers about, had shattered Saphron's heart, his betrayal leading to her untimely death. The story darkens with the wrath of Saphron's mother, Celeste, whose grief and rage birthed a curse, so vile and unyielding that it trapped my uncle's soul. Madam Claire's voice trembles as she describes the cruel brilliance of the enchantment.

She informs me that the reversal of such an intricate curse hinges on forgiveness and cooperation. Her brow furrows as she reveals that our families, each wounded by the other's actions, must come together and work as one to end not only the curse, but the darkness which keeps each family from finding closure. Celeste was certain such unity would never come to pass, believing she had successfully guaranteed my uncle's eternal torment.

Softly but with great resolve Madam Claire states, "We muss begin, not as reluctant allies, but as kindred spirits seekin' redemption, not jus' for ourselves, but also for da families. To undo dis, we muss call forth Celeste's memories and retrace her steps. We are 'bout to embark upon a journey which will not be easy, and it will demand more of us den either may be prepared to give." She leans closer, her gray eyes grow dark, locking onto mine. "But first child, forgiveness muss be given, and dis may prove the most challengin' of all tasks, as it muss include Celeste as well."

Her words linger, heavy with truth, as the oil lamps in the room seem to flicker in agreement. This is no ordinary undertaking; it will be a reckoning, not only with the past but with the fractured legacies of two families bound by love, loss, and vengeance.

The Séance

We talk for hours, not just about the tragedy that binds us together, but our lives, past and present. We speak of raw truths, the ones that have not only shaped, but haunted both our families for decades. Madam Celeste's voice softens as she speaks of Saphron, her eyes lighting up with pride as she recalls the woman her granddaughter became. But when she mentions her daughter, Celeste, her tone suddenly shifts, a quiet sorrow lacing her words. She will not delve too deeply into their relationship, she will only say that after Saphron's passing, something between them fractured, something irreparable.

I, too, speak of the pain that lingers in my family, and how Uncle Ray's disappearance sent my mother into a downward spiral, as she turned to alcohol for the comfort, we, as her family, failed to provide. I tell Madam Claire that even though my mother overcame her battle with alcohol, the emotional scars left by her brother's disappearance remain, and that is why I am here, to find the answers that have illuded our family for so long.

As if on cue, once I finish speaking, Madam Claire rises slowly from her chair and beckons me to follow her. "De time has come, child; the midnight hour is close at hand."

I walk slowly behind her down a dim hallway to a doorway adorned with a beaded curtain. A wave of cold air envelopes us as we step into the room; the only light coming from a ring of candles, their flames jumping erratically, casting strange silhouettes along the walls. The smoke from burning incense spirals through the air, weaving a veil of mystery and discernment. Other than bookcases and a few shelves, the room is devoid of furniture except for a round table standing at the center, draped in lace, with two wooden chairs facing each other. Madam Claire asks me to sit in the chair farthest from the door. Wrapping her shawl tightly around her shoulders, she lowers herself into the seat opposite mine. Something else is here, not just her physical form, but a palpable aura surrounding her. An odd sensation creeps over me. Am I hearing her thoughts? Her lips are not moving but I swear the words, "Do not worry, I commune wit' forces beyond mortal comprehension all da time," echoes soothingly in my mind.

She breaks the eerie silence.

"We are here to find da truth that'll lead us to yo Uncle Ray, an' figure out dat curse holdin' him," she says, her voice steady but heavy, like it's carrying years of family tradition. "If one is used for revenge, an' dependin' on what kind it is, da price for help from da Loa can be high."

Madam Claire takes a moment, and I can see her eyes grow distant, like she's remembering something painful.

"My daughter Celeste knew da risks of callen' down a curse like dat on yo uncle, but her grief was too much. It pushed her to make a choice dat ended up taken' her life. She couldn't deal wit' losin' Saphron, an' da guilt of what she did to yo uncle ate her up inside. Her health started fallen' apart, an' no doctor could explain what was happenin' to her. In da end, wit' da Loa's help, she joined her daughter an' the rest of da family who passed on."

"I don't agree wit' what Celeste did," she admits, her voice softening now. "But I understand why she did it. Grief, it muddies yo thoughts, yo mind, yo heart, an' yo soul. It make yuh do things yuh never thought yuh'd do. What matters now is dis: yuh an' I gotta come together, wit' open hearts, an' fix dis. Breakin' dat curse will bring peace to all involved, in both worlds, da spectral an' livin'."

"It's time to start, child," she says softly. "What yuh gonna see an' experience is gonna frighten yuh. Jus' know I am here wit yuh an' won't let nothin' bad happen."

She starts with a soft incantation, her words lyrical and rhythmic, carrying an energy that makes the room itself seem to vibrate. Shadows dance ominously across the walls to unheard melodies and twist around us as if they themselves are alive. The temperature in the room plummets, and I watch as our breaths escape, becoming visibly pale plumes in the dim light, like ghostly clouds suspended in the stillness, carrying along with them our unspoken words. A shiver runs through me. Sheer terror takes hold, and I cannot move.

And it begins.

A faint glow hovers above the center of the table. We watch as it becomes brighter, unfurling until the silhouette of a woman emerges, weak at first, then swelling as it grows larger until the light reveals Celeste's luminous and glimmering image. Her features are hazy at first, yet even in death, she is undeniably beautiful. Her dreadlocks appear weightless as they float carelessly above her shoulders, framing a face both fierce and sorrowful.

Her eyes burn like embers, piercing through time itself. When she speaks, her voice reverberates with echoes layered in anger and pain.

"You call upon me," she hisses. "You stir emotional wounds that have never healed."

I freeze, the chill seeping into my very bones, but Madam Claire remains calm.

"My misguided child," she says, her voice tinged with both sorrow and authority.

"We seek peace for yuh an' Saphron. We ask yuh to show us where yo pain began. Reveal to us da truth dat binds both yo souls in everlastin' torment."

Celeste's blazing eyes shoot ethereal bolts of energy at us, her fury palpable. Then, an unholy moan fills the house, shaking the walls. Objects crash to the floor, and the candles begin to burn brighter, their flames growing higher and twisting violently. I grip the edge of the table, my heart pounding against my ribs.

The room dissolves around us as we, along with Celeste, become part of a distant and frightening memory. We suddenly are absorbed into a new world as the curtain between the spirit and mortal world is being torn away.

We find ourselves in a cemetery. The wind howls through the ancient trees and crumbling tombs, carrying with it the scent of damp earth, serving as a dank reminder that we are witnessing an event from long ago. We are mere apparitions in a landscape shrouded by mist and moonlight. Before us, Celeste stands steady, her grief raw and jagged as she faces a marble statue. It bears my uncle's likeness, his face contorted in anguish, his arms solid stone and stretching outward, pleading for release. Celeste's expression remains cold and unyielding.

Clutching a vile to her chest before throwing it at the feet of the statue, Celeste raises her voice, reciting an incantation for all Loas to hear. Her words drip with heartbreak, sorrow, and wrath, weaving themselves into the mist. They are the threads which bind the spell as it wraps around his stone figure and seep into the earth beneath.

"You will watch over her grave," she chants, her voice trembling with unbridled emotion.

The cemetery itself seems to recoil, the ground trembling as the curse takes root. Her grief, raw and jagged, hangs in the air like a storm on the verge of breaking.

Her final cry shatters the silence, a wail of true mourning and defiance echoing into the depths of my soul.

Then, as suddenly as it began, the vision collapses into darkness, and we find ourselves back in Madam Claire's dimly lit room. The silhouette of her daughter lingers for a moment longer, her blazing eyes the last to fade. Silence follows, heavy and suffocating, as if the room needs time to recover from the apparition's presence.

Madam Claire slumps in her chair, her breath unsteady. The weight of her daughter's deed settles heavily on her, deepening the etched lines on her face, each one a testament to the exhaustion she must be feeling.

"He is dare," she whispers at last, her voice hoarse but unwavering. "In our family cemetery."

She takes a deep and haggard breath.

"Yuh have to believe I did not know yo' uncle was dare, child. Celeste never revealed to me what happened until the day she passed and den all she said is she used our craft to curse da man who stole her daughter's life, never sayin' more dan dat."

Madam Claire reaches across the table and grabs my hand.

"Yo' uncle, has been dare all dese years. I saw the stone figure when we buried Celeste, but honestly boy, jus' thought it was a statue put dare by mistake. Celeste never told us what she did wit your uncle. I never thought she had da power for such a spell. She muss have convinced da Loa and offered quite a reward for its help."

Taking a deep breath, she says she believes that Celeste's curse was twofold, a punishment and a demand for reconciliation and forgiveness.

"She has left us wit' one last ultimatum. Forged in pain, it consumed her soul so deeply dat she sacrificed herself, her happiness, an' even her life, believin' dat our two families would never come together to undo the curse."

Prior to this evening, I was unaware of how deeply all of this affected everyone involved. Correcting this injustice will not only allow my uncle's soul to rest, but Celeste and Saphron's as well. Fate brought me here to Madam Claire to undo a terrible mistake made by a mother whose heartbreak led to vigilante justice. Tonight however, in Celeste's voice and above the sorrow, I think I may have heard a tinge of remorse and regret for what she had done.

Once we regain our strength, I help Madam Claire extinguish the candles one by one, plunging the room into near-darkness. Our only source of light now is the faint glow of streetlights from outside slowly seeping in through the curtains. As we stand, the weight of the séance lingers like an unseen tether, binding us to an unspoken promise that we make to each other without a word needing to be uttered.

"We have much to do, child." Her eyes meet mine, and for the first time, I truly understand the enormity of the task ahead of us.

Tomorrow night, by the light of the moon, we will confront the curse as we congregate among the tombstones and mist that carries the echoes of the past. Redemption for my uncle is only the beginning. The ritual we must perform will bring closure to not only him, but all generations, past and present. At last, the wounds of yesterday will have the chance to heal.

After I help Madam Claire pick up the items Celeste's spirit caused to fall to the floor, the time has come for me to leave. Once done tidying up the room, Madam Claire asks if I am okay. I assure her that I am shaken but alright. She wishes me good night as she escorts me out.

With a heavy sigh I step into the darkness of early morning, an indescribable chill still clinging to me despite the warm air. Before beginning my walk home, I rest on Madam Claire's front door stoop and try hard to process what I just witnessed. In all my years of research and planning for this day, I could never have convinced my younger self that voodoo, spells and these strange rituals could be real, but here I sit, witness to things most people never have the chance to experience, and I do not know whether to feel honored or cursed.

That was intense, keeps running through my mind. In a daze,

I rise to leave. My feet carry me back home as the walk back allows me to reflect on what I just experienced. Though I learned a lot more about what happened to Uncle Ray, there is so much left unknown.

Tomorrow marks the end of our journey; one I still feel unprepared to embark upon. What I know about Celeste is little, and I can sense there's much more at play here than mere retribution. This goes far deeper than a mother's heartache and grief. There is something far darker. I find myself wishing I could understand why Celeste sentenced my uncle to such a cruel fate.

Madam Celeste's Vengeful Plan

I have devised a plan. One in which I intend to ensnare the man responsible for my little girl's death. I was told he likes to frequent a bar in the Quarter called *Jazz Note*. That is where our paths will cross, and his undoing will begin. Before we meet, I must not forget to light a candle and say a prayer to Lenglensou, our patron saint of justice, and protector of our sacred traditions. He is not only a guardian; he is a vengeful Loa known for exacting revenge on the unentitled ones. I will need his guidance and power to make right an unforgivable wrong.

I know it to be dangerous, using our sacred religion for revenge, and asking such favors can be costly. However, justice calls louder than my conscience and I am prepared to pay any price the spirits may demand.

Saphron, my only daughter, is gone. Her light, laughter and promise, all extinguished by the ambition of a deceitful reporter. He wormed his way into her life, seducing her with empty promises and asking her to reveal secrets he had no right to know. She loved and trusted him in her innocent way, sharing pieces of our craft out of naivete, only to be cast aside once he had taken from her all he could. With no regret, he left her, showing no concern, while her fragile heart surrendered to sorrow.

The memory of how I found her still haunts me. I knocked on her door that morning. She did not answer. After my third attempt to wake her, I enter the room and immediately see her delicate lifeless body crumpled on the floor beside her canopy bed. Her frail heart, weakened since birth, could not bear his betrayal. To this day, the pain of her loss burns within me like an unquenchable fire.

Now, as the candle's flame dances in the cranberry red bubble glass globe on the table of the Jazz Note bar, I sit in the shadows. My thirst for justice is fueled by the red wine I sip. The soft and soulful tones being played by the band ease my angry spirit as I wait patiently for fate to bring him to me. Tonight, my gaze will not waver from the door as my heart pounds with the rhythm of vengeance long in the making.

As expected, he finally saunters into the club, shaking off the evening's chill. I am prepared. He exudes a dark aura with unwarranted confidence feeding his arrogance. His insufferable grin falters as our eyes meet. He does not know me but soon will.

He chooses a table near mine. *Good, he is directly in my line of sight.* I sit poised, my wardrobe chosen purposely, ensuring I stand out just enough. He is a man driven by greed and curiosity; a dangerous combination I will use against him. My signals must be subtle and deliberate as I remain mysterious yet approachable.

I bide my time as he nurses his first drink. Eventually, he will revisit the bar and that is when my carefully laid plan will come to fruition. As he passes my table on his way for a fresh, cold beer, I "accidentally" brush his hand, whispering beneath my breath, an incantation meant to ensnare his curiosity and draw his attention.

The spell is successful, as I feel a shift in his aura. His focus and curiosity will gradually turn towards me. I have set the trap, however, there's something or someone else, another inhabitant. Not a spirit I recognize, but perhaps a soul that is out of place or not of this time. Within him is a presence, lingering, and confused. It remains unseen, even to me, yet undeniable. I sense he himself is unaware of this visitor.

He returns to his table. Occasionally, he glances in my direction, and I feign indifference. Patience is not a strong suit of mine, but tonight I use it as one of my weapons.

When the moment is right, I rise from my chair and glide toward the powder room, ensuring my movements command attention without betraying my intent. Upon my return, I stealthfully walk up behind him and lean close to his ear and in a determined whisper, request that he bring me a drink so we can talk.

Unable to resist my request, he brings me a glass of wine and introduces himself. He asks if he can join me. I give permission to both him and his unseen visitor to sit. As soon as he takes his seat, I can no longer sense two souls, only his. I guess his companion spirit had somewhere else it needed to be.

He attempts to be charming but is unable to mask his greed. I am certain he is using the same well practiced lines as he did with my little girl. With pride, he introduces himself as a reporter from Ohio, sent here to write an article about New Orleans and Mardi Gras. He speaks of the beauty of the city and how he has become enthralled with a culture he never knew existed, stating he would like to learn more about that side of New Orleans. He tries to convince me that sharing this knowledge will add a new depth and another layer of interest for his readers.

I am a stranger to him but have asked around and found out exactly who he is and what he is all about. He wastes his words on me but will not speak outright about his ambitions or what it is that he seeks. Dropping not-so-subtle hints, he tries to flatter and charm me. I grow deeply disgusted but must hide my detest for him if I am to be successful. Slowly I gain his confidence carefully weaving my web, spinning stories I know he wants to hear. He is interested in becoming acquainted with the Loa. It becomes obvious that Saphron explained that the Loa are the saints we pray to who often grant us power to protect those we love. He speaks of his desire to know more about the darker side of our religion. He dances around his intentions and will not ask outright about the rituals and incantations meant for vengeance, though I know that to be the reason he is here.

The community has told me of his interest in locating someone to help him become involved in our religion. That is my sole purpose for being here tonight. I intend to give the ambitious man what he seeks, someone who will show and teach him more about voodoo than he ever dreamed. I look at the little man and chuckle to myself, *you have no idea dear boy. Soon you will learn all you need to know about voodoo, retribution, and more.* As practitioners we keep our secrets within our own circle for many reasons. First and foremost is the respect and understanding you must have regarding our religious practices.

I sit quietly as he attempts to impress me with stories of his life back in Cincinnati. Sipping my wine, I listen patiently using deliberate gestures along with whispered spells to maintain his interest and my control over him. I need this opportunity to thoroughly ensnare this unsuspecting outsider. He remains unaware there is a purpose in every motion I make.

Wanting him to believe he has succeeded in gaining my trust, I present him with a gris-gris bag, explaining that the spices, oils and ground bones it holds have been blessed and will bring him success. However, that is a lie. It has been prayed over to ensure the bond we have formed tonight remains strong. His eyes gleam with avarice as he takes the bag from my hand, now completely confident he has won me over.

With the trap set, we meet for several nights, and I use this time to draw him in deeper, teaching him minor spells and rituals, always holding back enough to keep him wanting more.

He has grown impatient, his hunger for power now consumes him. I explain that the gift he desires can only be attained through patience, honor and respect, reminding him that it has taken my family generations to perfect our craft.

At last, the time has come. I offer him the ultimate prize, a prayer so potent that it will grant him the power he craves. He agrees to meet me tomorrow as I explain the ritual must take place at midnight in our family cemetery, where our ancestral power is at its strongest. I tell him the spirits of my family must grant permission for him to receive such a rare blessing. His eager and hungry eyes betray him as I continue to smile and conceal my vengeance, while his excitement and exuberance gnaws at the depths of my soul.

The cemetery will serve as the stage for my ultimate revenge, a place where righteousness and vengeance will intertwine. I remind myself, *this is all to make right what happened to my little girl Saphron, for whom justice has been denied.*

A Mother's Revenge

The midnight air clings heavily to the land thick with anticipation. I stand in the center of our family cemetery, beneath a canopy of cypress trees whose moss-slung limbs sway like mournful ghosts in the humid breeze. Every stone, every shadow, every crypt, echoes of our ancestors' souls whispering through the night. This place is sacred to us, and tonight, it will serve as the stage for overdue retribution.

I am here to rectify a wrong perpetrated upon my family. Losing my daughter Saphron leaves a gaping hole in my life, her laughter, once a melody, is now painfully silent. Taken from this world by someone who exploited her, my naïve young daughter fell for a man whose hunger for power was greater than his love for her. He used her to gain access to our family's knowledge of the sacred voodoo that runs through our blood. And for that, he must pay.

I raise my hands to the heavens. Using a deliberate low tone to recite the incantatory chant, I call on the spirits of my ancestors to awaken and bear witness to this ceremony. In the night's fog, they stir, rising from their peaceful graves, their presence electrifying the air. They answer my call, their collective energy building as they join me in implementing my carefully crafted plan.

"Tonight, we restore our honor," I whisper to them, my voice thick with grief and vengeance.

"We correct a wrong that can no longer be ignored. Tonight, we gather to deliver punishment to the one who stole Saphron's life."

As I speak, I feel a subtle shift of the air surrounding this sacred stage alerting me to the arrival of our guest of honor. As directed, he appears on time. From the shadows the man who destroyed my daughter's world, walks with hopeful purpose. His silhouette, backlit by the moon, makes him seem almost angelic, but I know better. The hunger in his eyes betrays his true nature.

He approaches; each step measured but unsure. He is unaware of the ghosts that follow him, unseen but ever-present, as they watch his every move. I can sense his heart race and see his ambition, written clearly on his face.

"Stop there," I command, my voice sharp, cutting through the thick, moist air.

"You need not come any farther. You will listen and do as you are told."

The spirits murmur around me, remaining unseen spectral whispers through the trees, as I begin the ritual. I draw a circle of ash and salt on the ground, which will serve as a portal between the living and the dead. My chant grows louder, a melody both beautiful and terrible, laced with deepest sorrow and burning vengeance. Around us, the tombstones flicker with an eerie, ethereal glow as the souls of my ancestors joined their voices to mine.

The reporter, hungry for power and a desperate fool, stands before me, his eyes wide with anticipation and fear. Confusion clouds his eyes; the events unfolding are a mystery he cannot yet grasp. He came here thinking he could control the power of the Loa, but he will learn how wrong he is.

"You seek power, child," I say softly, stepping closer to him.

"But power always demands a price."

His eager nod tells me everything I need to know. I see the undeniable arrogance in his eyes as he speaks.

"I couldn't resist your offer."

I retrieve a vial from my satchel, which contains a thick, dark liquid that is offensively pungent to the nose. His gaze locks onto it, and I know he can feel the pull of the magic. He hungers for what he believes it can give him.

"Is this what you desire, dear boy?" I ask.

"Yes," he whispers, his voice trembling.

"This potion will bring to us clarity and satisfaction," I say, pouring the liquid into a shallow bowl.

"But you must accept this without question. Do you understand?"

His hands shake as he nods, the word "yes," barely audible as it escapes his lips.

I wave my hand over the bowl, muttering the word "Jistis," which makes the liquid glow faintly. His eyes widen, and I watch with joy as his body trembles in anticipation. My ancestor's ghostly voices rise as they harmonize with my chant. The ritual aids in drawing him deeper into my carefully woven and inescapable web, that is now charged with our family's power.

With a smile, I hand him the bowl which once ingested, will deliver to him a potion he believes will bring him abilities few other men have received.

His brow furrows at the foul odor coming from the shallow bowl. The liquid, still luminous, shines on his face, enhancing the look in his eyes as he hungrily drinks the potion.

I step back momentarily, giving the potion time to course through his body, his eyes growing wider as he does not understand what is taking place.

"What I need now, dear boy, is to know, do you feel remorse for what you did to Saphron?"

At the mention of her name, his face drains of color, his hands dropping the bowl to the ground. It shatters at his feet.

His voice, unable to hide the fear now overtaking him, asks, "How do you know that name?"

I step closer, my eyes locking with his, steady and unyielding. "Because I am her mother," I say, my voice low but resolute. "And tonight, you will answer for what you did to her."

I watch as the realization strikes him like an unexpected blow to the gut. His eyes fill with fear as he begins to understand that, for him, time has now run out and there can be no escape. The consequences for the ritual have already begun as the ghosts of my ancestors rise around us, flickering in the shadows. The man's body stiffens as the potion takes effect; his hands tremble as if the very air is choking him.

"Please," he begs, his voice cracking. "I didn't ... I didn't mean to..."

"You didn't love her," I hiss, the venom in my voice rising. "Nor did you cherish her. You, my boy, destroyed her."

The spirits of my family stir, their energies now swirling in the air like a storm ready to break. His breath grows short, able now to only take ragged gasps.

"Look at me, child," I command as I step forward, forcing him to meet my gaze. "Look into my eyes and you will see the soul of the daughter you stole from me."

His eyes widen in horror as he realizes he can do nothing to stop what is happening. The time has come. Vengeance is at hand. As the ritual nears its climax, the stars vanish from the sky, causing the darkness to pulse, and the air thickens from the energy being produced by the angry souls who surround us. Lightning splits the sky, illuminating the cemetery. My ancestors are now completely visible to him in the night's fog, their spectral forms glowing as their faces fill with fury.

He screams, but the sound catches in his throat, unable to escape, instead only a guttural sound crosses his lips. I step back, my voice final as it resonates with the power of our ancestors. I raise my arms to the heavens and throw my head back as I speak the last phrase of the curse, "Revanche pou Saphron."

He gasps for breath, but no words come. The spirits gather, encircling the little man, and I watch as their spectral glow casts light upon his body slowly turning to stone. His eyes wide with terror as the end nears and his form hardens, silencing his voice forever.

His last breath is a whisper, a pathetic attempt at an apology. "I couldn't love her like she wanted me to … Please try to understand, I am…"

His words stop there. He can no longer speak.

Tonight, his soul will be lost to time, and he will remain a forgotten echo serving as a sentinel for my daughter for all eternity.

Now that justice has been done, and the sins of the living finally resolved, my ancestors can return to their slumber never to be disturbed again. I watch in silent reverence as each soul's shimmering light drifts back beneath the soil of their individual plots and mausoleums, fading into the night. Quietly I say my farewell as I sink to the ground exhausted, my back finding the gnarled oak which stands steadfast over Saphron's grave.

In the moments before dawn breaks over this hallowed ground, a pale fog rises above the horizon, washing away tonight's depravity. Silence now reclaims this sacred place as justice wavers between vengeance and forgiveness.

When Things Become Too Real

The very first thing on my agenda this morning is to stop at the boarding house, grab my camera and flag a cab down. Knowing the cemetery's location, I'm eager to see my uncle's weathered and stony figure with my own eyes. I need photos for my article and as evidence to myself that I am not losing my mind.

As the cab rattles down the gravel road, unease creeps in. My palms sweat as I clutch the camera bag on my lap. I have no exact location, no map, no guarantee I'll even find the statue we saw during the séance. Doubt fills my mind. Even though I know all this is real, somewhere, deep in the back of my mind, I keep telling myself to wake up.

When we reach the cemetery gates, the driver asks if I would like him to wait. I shake my head, explaining I am unsure how long it will take to complete my task. With that he speeds away, disappearing down the road. The air here is heavy, damp, and strong with the scent of moss. The sprawling burial sites feel like an endless maze of above-ground mausoleums and weathered headstones.

The séance had shown me only glimpses of Saphron's grave and my uncle's statue beside a tree draped in Spanish moss. As I wander, I realize, with so little information, I am going into this search blind. I stumble several times as I walk past the Cedar and cypress trees that dominate the landscape, their roots breaking through cracked stone paths. In all the visions I have experienced, a large gnarled old oak tree provides shade over Madam Claire's family plot. I have seen no such trees from my vantage point. As the hours drag on, my legs begin to grow tired.

Then, just as I consider giving up, a loud crack shatters the silence. I whip around, heart pounding, to see an old oak swaying in the distance, a freshly broken branch sprawled at its base. Could it be? My pulse quickens as I rush toward the sound, stumbling in haste and slipping on the wet ground.

The nearer I get, the more certain I become. The tree's Spanish moss-covered twisted limbs match the one I have seen so many times before. And there, beneath its shadow, stands a stony figure. My breath catches as I slowly approach. There can be no doubt, I am looking at the likeness of my uncle standing sentinel over a grave, his chiseled face frozen, showing him in mid-peril.

I glance at the headstone he silently guards. The name, carved in delicate script, sends a chill down my spine: **Saphron Mink**. In reverence, I remove my uncle's fedora and bow my head in prayer.

"Saphron," I whisper, "I'm so sorry for everything."

Turning to the statue, I study it closely. Even after so many years and beneath layers of dirt and decay, it's him alright. Every detail matches the visions that have been haunting me, the tilt of his head, the crease of his suit, the solemn set of his jaw. My throat tightens as I formally introduce myself.

"Uncle Ray," I say, my voice trembling.

"So very nice to meet you at last. You've been a mystery my entire life. I'm not here to judge you, but I need you to understand how your choices have not only affected but also hurt everyone who loved you." I pause, taking a shaky breath. "Regardless, I forgive you and I hope by the end of all this, everyone else will."

I raise my camera, the lens trembling slightly as I focus on the statue standing before me. I take many photographs, circling my uncle, making certain to capture every angle. These photos will serve as evidence and indisputable proof that the man who disappeared so long ago is here, trapped in stone.

Feeling I have taken all the pictures I can, I lower the camera and reach out. My fingers graze the cold, rough surface of his hand. A shiver runs through me. It feels like stone, but an energy lies beneath it, faint but undeniable.

"We're going to free you, Madam Claire and I. That is my promise to you."

The wind stirs, and for a moment, the air feels alive charged with unseen forces. I step back, giving the statue one last look.

"I'll be back soon, I promise."

As I turn to leave, a chill sweeps over me, and for a fleeting moment, I feel as though I am being watched.

And there he is, my faithful companion, swooping in to join me. He lands on my uncle's cold, stiff arm.

"Found him," he says.

"Yes," I answer, wiping an unexpected tear from my eye. "Ready to go home?" I ask. He does not answer.

I turn to leave, and a harsh and uncomfortable silence follows me as I walk toward the entrance. My mind buzzes with thoughts of what is to come. Reaching the cemetery gates, I look up and am surprised to see a cab with its motor running.

With a bewildered look on my face, the driver rolls down his window and asks if I am Eddie.

"Yes, I am," I answer with great confusion.

"Sent here by Madam Claire," he shouts. "Said you would

be out of here about three o'clock."

Taking out my pocket watch, I reply, "well, I am only five minutes late,"

As I reach for the door handle, he lets me know in no uncertain terms my crow cannot ride along.

"You go ahead, I'll meet you at home," I advise my new best friend.

He caws and flies off, but not before leaving a present for the driver on the windshield.

"Sorry," I say. "I'll get out and clean that off for you. He can be a little vindictive when he feels slighted."

With an audible huff, the driver says, "don't bother," as he turns on the windshield wipers, washing away the offending droppings, saying nothing else as he pulls away from the cemetery.

Arriving at the boarding house, I pay the cab driver and give him a hefty tip as an apology for my winged friend. I exit the car quickly and shake my index finger at the bird sitting patiently on the black iron fence surrounding the house. "You cost me another ten dollars, you flying rat."

He glares at me, cawing loudly in protest as I enter the house.

Was it His Soul or Just a Dream?

By the time I reach my room, the stillness feels oppressive. My faithful companion sits on the windowsill outside, patiently waiting, but not speaking. I place a handful of trail mix out for him and ask if he wants to go with me into the Quarter for a bite to eat. He caws, and I take it as a yes. After a late lunch/early dinner, we spend thirty minutes walking around, but I grow tired. I will need to sleep soon, as I am meeting Madam Claire later this evening.

Too tired to walk back to the boarding house, I hail a cab, but my little buddy is having none of it, as he swoops down, pecking at my head. "Shoo," I say, brushing him away. But he is insistent, so I signal for the car to leave without me. "What is your problem?" I ask the crow rhetorically. "I am tired and really do not feel like walking." He does not answer. I can only surmise he wants company on his journey back to the boardinghouse.

The walk home is uneventful as the bird flies just a short distance ahead of me. Arriving at the front door, I knock the mud from my shoes before entering. I glance up at my companion and I tell him, "I'll meet you upstairs."

The weather today is unseasonably mild, and the room is comfortable for which I am grateful. I try to rest, but my overactive mind will not allow it, as though it knows there are unsettling visions waiting on the other side.

With a sigh of resignation, I close my eyes, and as feared, a creeping sense of unease fills the air, as my mind succumbs to a chilly descent into the unknown. Behind closed eyelids, my Uncle Ray appears, his face illuminated by a pale, unflattering glow. He makes a motion for me to follow. His voice is familiar yet somehow foreign, "Walk with me, nephew," he says softly. "I have some things to share with you." I want to resist, to force myself awake, but something stronger holds me back, as I feel trapped in his gaze. Is this a dream or am I really standing here with my uncle?

With all I have learned and experienced these past few days, and especially with what I witnessed last night during the séance Madam Claire performed, I am no longer certain what is real anymore.

Everything feels blurred. The lines between the tangible and the spectral dissolve into a thick fog as a sense of unease takes over my being. Unable to fight any longer, I surrender, allowing myself to descend into the vision, and follow Uncle Ray across a ghostly expanse.

He speaks of things from his and my mother's childhood and how he was always the black sheep of the family. Unlike the rest, he says he was more bookish and very much a loner. He explains his need to explore and understand different cultures, believing that the more you know about the world around you, the better you can interact with your fellow human beings.

"All this," he says, "Leads us to where we are now."

He explains he wishes to reveal just how and why he came to be encased in marble, forever cursed to stand vigil over young Saphron's grave.

Ahead, I see a familiar sight. Uncle Ray has brought me to his effigy.

I want to tell him that during the unsettling séance, I watched in horror as he became entrapped in stone, cursed by Saphron's mother's distain and vengeance. At this moment, I realize this is his tale to tell, so quietly I listen standing shoulder to shoulder with the apparition of my uncle. As we stare at his lifeless form in front of us, he begins to explain the weight and gravity of his story.

Uncle Ray reveals an epic saga of love, loss and betrayal.

Shrouded in an air of mystery, Uncle Ray's life was a captivating mix of alluring charm and carefully guarded secrets, leaving those around him constantly questioning what they knew about him. Reduced to a stone figure, he now stands as a chilling testament to pain and unspoken anguish.

"This punishment," he points towards the statue, "was born of Saphron's mother, whose grief and wrath knew no bounds."

He explains that her family believed his connection with Saphron Mink was a calculated attempt to exploit their voodoo secrets for personal gain.

"But the truth," he continues, "is bitter and tangled like knotted barbed wire, and painfully heartbreaking."

Even if this is more than just a dream, I am glad Uncle Ray's spirit has come to me, sharing images of his past. His words fill my mind, painting a picture of a man who hid his true self behind carefully constructed walls. He shares with me the driving force behind his turn to voodoo. It was not power or ambition, but a painful, gut-wrenching heartache which left him hollow. He sought revenge against Michael, the man who had broken his heart and left him longing for a life that, because of his chosen profession, he could never fully embrace.

Uncle Ray lived in constant fear of public ridicule and the possibility of losing his career as a journalist should anyone ever discover his "alternative" lifestyle. Michael was everything to

Uncle Ray, but their relationship occurred in the early 80s and 90s, a time when living openly as a gay man could destroy a career, reputation, or even one's life. Fears such as those kept my uncle in the shadows while Michael longed to live proud and out loud. When Ray refused to risk everything for a love he was afraid to claim, Michael ended the relationship, leaving my uncle emotionally empty and bitter.

He would use the assignment which brought him to The Crescent City twofold, first, to get over his failed relationship and second, to learn more about and enjoy a city known for its party atmosphere. By stumbling into the wrong voodoo shop, he would learn of curses, charms and voodoo. In his despair, Uncle Ray would turn to these practices seeking a spell to curse Michael, not to harm him, but to burden him with misfortune. A broken heart can make you contemplate many things, and Uncle Ray's first instinct was retribution against Michael. He heard whispers of voodoo magic, spells and charms that would allow the average person to use potions for love or retaliation. He decided to seek out such places and learn all he could about this intriguing side of New Orleans.

He would meet Saphron in one of the more authentic voodoo shops, he tells me, and she would become an unexpected complication. To obtain knowledge and learn more about voodoo curses and incantations, Uncle Ray allowed her to believe he shared her affections. By the time he realized just how deep this young woman's feelings for him were, it was too late. As a young voodoo apprentice with bright eyes and an open heart, she saw in Ray what he refused to see in himself, a man worthy of love. She meant well, but was casting her emotions upon someone who could not return them.

He knew he had to end things with Saphron gently. He first started by using a lie which had worked well with all other relationships he began with women. But Saphron saw through it, accusing him of toying with her emotions. When he finally tried to tell her the truth, confessing his love for another man, she refused to believe him.

"You don't talk, look or act that way," she said. "In this city,

I've known plenty, and they're all flamboyant, with a flair for style and fashion. You're not like that."

Unable to accept his reality and apology, her fragile heart broke. Combined with the strain of her congenital heart condition, and emotionally unable to bear the pain, she would pass away that very night.

Saphron had informed her mother she had met a reporter a few weeks earlier and that even though he lived far away, she unintentionally started growing fond of him. Because of the age and race barrier Saphron chose not to reveal more about the relationship she had engaged in. Saphron was upset when she came home that night and her mother did not notice the bloodshot eyes and tear-stained cheeks which adorned her daughter's face, a regret she would carry with her for the rest of her days. Saphron quietly exiled herself to her room, not wishing to answer any questions as to why she was upset. Celeste was a loving yet strict and judgmental mother and that night, Saphron was in no mood for an "I told you so."

The following morning Celeste found Saphron's lifeless body lifeless on the bedroom floor. This is when a mother's grief curdled, festering into rage. Blinded by vengeance and pain, she blamed Uncle Ray for her daughter's death. She would devise a plan to lure him to their family cemetery, where she could lie upon him a curse to stand as a guardian for all eternity over Saphron's grave.

I watch as Uncle Ray shows me what happened to him on his last night.

With her carefully laid plans coming to fruition, Celeste patiently waits for the man who caused her daughter's untimely demise. The ritual, a mere few minutes of hushed incantations and grief fueled gestures, concludes, yet the repercussions stretch on for years.

For the second time in as many days, I am bearing witness to my uncle's demise.

As his body hardens, and the stone creeps over his flesh, Uncle Ray tries desperately to speak the words he has never dared say aloud to anyone other than Saphron. He wants desperately to apologize to Celeste and her family. "I couldn't love her the way she wanted me to. I am…"

But the curse silences him before he can complete his confession. The word he has carried under his breath his entire life "…gay," now lost to the stillness, leaves him forever suspended in a moment of unfinished truth.

Having to remain silent for so many years regarding his "secret life," I am honored Uncle Ray feels comfortable enough to share his past with me, but I have to wonder, *is this real? Is this the soul of my uncle seeking closure? Or is this just a cruel trick by my subconscious to weave his tragedy into the fogginess of my exhaustion.*

Today, the answers to these questions are unimportant. What does matter, are the truths he can no longer speak aloud. It now falls on me to set him and his words free.

Uncle Ray's Torment

Saphron feared the ramifications of revealing to me her family's long history with voodoo and the occult. But now, my insistence to learn those secrets will become my torment, remaining etched into my being by the curse her mother will invoke.

Standing before me is a scorned mother, her real identity, I did not know, but fate will now properly introduce us. All too late I realize what is happening.

Madam Celeste has successfully seduced me into this nightmare. Far more than a knowledgeable voodoo priestess, I refused to acknowledge the many red flags that were there all along. My greed blinded me, and I have allowed myself to be lured here under false pretenses. Her promise was to gift me with abilities, few outsiders, as she calls us, have ever known.

Her once kind voice is no more, instead it is filled with venom and sorrow as it echoes through the fog, binding me in her grief and rage. Her graceful movements have been replaced by angry and erratic gestures, my mind silently screams, coming here tonight may have been a mistake.

This grieving woman is beyond angry. Her heart is broken beyond repair. She accuses me of not loving or treasuring Saphron but she is mistaken. No one will know how much that precious young girl meant to me. How do you tell a grieving mother how sorry you are for breaking the heart of her little girl? How do you tell her, you never meant to lead her daughter on, but because of who you are, you could never return the innocent young girl's misplaced love. When I revealed to Saphron why we could never be together, she did not believe me and because of that, I am responsible for her weakened heart failing. It is too late now for apologies.

In the silence, I can hear her final words ringing in my ears. I want to scream, to beg for mercy, but am unable. I try to fight against my fate but can no longer move as my body slowly begins turning to marble. My legs stiffen and my skin hardens as it slowly transforms into cold and unyielding rock. As her curse on me takes full hold, I feel the weight of my sins press down on me, heavy like the stone I am becoming. There are certain Creole and Cajun words I do not comprehend, but through her incantations I hear, "You will stand as a sentinel, gazing upon the daughter you took from me. Allow her tombstone to be a chilling reminder that your actions extinguished her beautiful light."

Once she has completed her ritual and the spirits of her family return to their resting places, she takes a ragged breath before letting out a grief ladened mournful wail which fills the cemetery. She does not turn to leave immediately, instead she rests beneath an old tree, crying as she asks her saints for forgiveness.

Morning dawns and I stand petrified as Madam Celeste exits the cemetery, head lowered and muttering, "It is done."

Saphron's spirit lingers, a constant reminder of what I have done. The echoes of her shattered heart and my guilt will tether me to this cemetery with invisible and unbreakable chains for all eternity.

I hear strange souls whisper as they surround me, and Saphron's presence is the loudest among them. Her eyes, once filled with hope and warmth, now burn with sorrow and betrayal. I see her soul flicker in the moonlight, hear her voice in the rustling wind, and feel her anguish in every howl and chill that pierces the foggy nights.

This is to be my torment. My soul, imprisoned in stone, forever haunted by the echoes of my betrayal.

The bitter taste of the reckless lies and deceit I allowed to doom both of us is to be a constant and hellish reminder of the souls I destroyed. I had betrayed her. I betrayed us both, and for eternity I will stand here tormented, longing for forgiveness I do not deserve.

Doubt Fills My Heart and Mind

The evening sun dips below the horizon, its fading light casting shadows across the pavement. Another humid night presses against me as I make my way to St. Roch Avenue, the dampness clinging to my skin. By the time I reach Madam Claire's door, I'm drenched, my breath heavy as anticipation and doubt fill my mind.

She greets me with a knowing look and guides me into the dimly lit séance room. The scent of burned sage and melted candle wax fills the air, mingling with a tension that feels almost alive. Tonight, I can see her shelves brim with talismans, aged books, and artifacts etched with symbols I cannot decipher. Listen closely enough, and you can hear the faint echoes of lives and loves past, their stories carried along the sweet air. Shadows from flickering candles dance as they encompass the room, their movements slow and concise, as if unseen eyes watch from every corner. The energy here is an unsettling contradiction; warm and soothing yet brimming with cold and unspoken power.

Madam Claire gestures towards the round mahogany table in the center of the room. The same one from last night, however this evening a colorful cloth adorned with strange, embroidered symbols replaces the fragile crocheted one from twenty-four hours ago. Her steely gray eyes meet mine, ageless and filled with wisdom I cannot begin to fathom. She moves with spiritual grace, her flowing robe laced with gold threads shimmering faintly in the candlelight. As she takes her seat across from me, a warm, incense-laden breeze stirs the air, carrying faint whispers of past chants and incantations along with it.

She smiles, soft and inviting, as if greeting an old friend.

"Sit," she says, her voice steady and soothing.

I obey, though unease coils tightly in my chest.

She arranges strange talismans on the table, her hands moving with practiced precision, every gesture deliberate.

"Yuh muss' understand," she says, not looking up, her voice blanketing the room with calm certainty,

"dis is not jus' 'bout belief in voodoo. It is 'bout openin' yuh heart to possibilities beyond what yuh know."

I nod, the weight of her words heavy with purpose as they settle quietly in my mind. From beneath the table, she brings out a small intricately carved wooden box.

"In here are relics from my family," she says, her tone gentle and kind.

"We need 'least one from yuh family. Did yuh bring wit' yuh da lock of Saphron's hair?"

From my pocket I slowly produce the cobalt blue vile. Knowing how much it meant to Uncle Ray; I wonder if I should even be doing this. I am having serious second thoughts. This all feels so right, yet so wrong.

Madam Claire senses my apprehension and nods knowingly, "it's okay," she reassures me. "It belonged to Saphron and yuh uncle. Cause of dis, it crosses both family lines, makin' it more important 'den yuh can know."

I place it in the box and then add the worn notepad I found just a few nights before, along with the black and white photograph of my uncle.

"Dese will guide the ancestors to us," she explains, arranging the items with great care. I hear her whisper strange words as she touches each one.

"Do yuh believe?" she asks, her voice steady, her focus unbroken.

The question slices through me. I pause for a moment before forcing a response.

"Yes."

She nods, satisfied.

"Belief is da first step toward acceptin' an' understandin' yo importance here."

My doubt must show because her sharp eyes catch it instantly.

"Yuh are uneasy," she observes, pouring tea from a delicate pot decorated with what I recognize to be ancient Haitian symbols.

"Dat is normal."

I accept the cup, inhaling the fragrant steam before sipping the brew.

"I don't know what to expect," I admit.

"Expectation is a human burden," she replies. "Tonight is 'bout intention and belief."

Her words settle over me, simple yet layered in meaning.

"Dis isn't jus' 'bout breakin' a curse," she continues. "Dis 'bout healin'. Forgiveness muss' be given freely, wit' out anger or blame. My daughter forged dis bond from pain an' betrayal, convinced it could never be lifted." Her gaze intensifies, locking onto mine. "Yuh are da key, young man."

"Why me?" I ask, my voice barely above a whisper.

"'Cause yuh heart carry no malice. Dat purity is essential, not jus' for yuh uncle, but for my daughter an' granddaughter too."

Her words ease my apprehension, laying bare a purpose I hadn't realized I carried. As doubt churns within me, a faint caw echoes from outside. I hear the familiar cry of my faithful winged shadow, his timing impeccable, as if he is urging me forward.

Madam Claire's voice lowers, her tone shifts, now grave and steady.

"We call upon spirits tonight. My ancestors will bear witness to our efforts to mend what hate an' betrayal have torn apart."

A chill races down my spine as my mind flashes back to the séance from last night. I will never forget the ghostly form she conjured and how angry and terrifying her daughter was, and now she is saying tonight we will witness even more angry spirits?

"Remember," she says, her fingers hovering over an ancient carved bone amulet. She mouths words I cannot hear before placing it in my hands, "pure hearts can cut through even da darkest magic. Keep dis close; it will protect an' calm yuh."

I place the amulet around my neck, its surface cool against my skin.

She leans closer, her voice low as it seems to carry the weight of generations.

"Voodoo isn't 'bout power taken or given. It is da energy an' belief we share. Though yuh are an outsider, yuh come wit pure respect and intentions which transcends origins."

Her words steady me, their certainty bridging the chasm between her belief and my doubt.

"We go to da cemetery tonight," she says, her tone shifts to soft and comforting.

"Da spirits, will understand we come wit' pure hearts, yearnin' for reconciliation. Once dey accept us, together we will break dis devastaten' curse."

Feeling frightened and apprehensive I inhale deeply. Madam Claire takes me by the arm. "It's time, we muss' prepare to leave."

Rising from the table she hands me the small wooden box. "Yuh hold on to dis for me will yuh Cher?" My hand quivers slightly as I take it from her, drawing it close to my chest. I handle it with care knowing it contains more than mere objects. I feel far more than just carved wood in my arms, there is a spiritual energy emanating from this old box of combined family heirlooms.

The Journey Nears Its End

The cab rattles down the gravel road, each bump jolting me deeper into the uneasy reality of our mission. Madam Claire sits beside me, her lips moving in a hushed, rhythmic whisper. I dare not interrupt. Her presence is a paradox, comforting in its wisdom yet deeply intimidating, like standing before an ancient, all-knowing oracle. In my lap rests the hand-carved box, its weight, a reminder that it holds the most important items for the ritual. What this box contains is not mere relics, they are symbols of two entwined families, bound by pain and sorrow. Separately, they hold no special power, but together, they represent hope and promise.

The cab driver, a wiry man with deep-set eyes, seems to understand what is about to happen better than I do. When Madam Claire recites the address of our destination, he touches a necklace made of beads and bones dangling from his mirror and gives a solemn nod. His quiet gesture sends chills through my soul. Without a word, he acknowledges what remains unspoken, that, together; we all share in a sacred pact.

As we arrive at the cemetery, the humidity diminishes. A stiff wind sweeps through the air, and clouds creep over the moon, cloaking the night in an eerie gray. Each step toward Madam Claire's family plot feels like I am wading through quicksand; the ground pulling at my feet as if reluctant to let me pass. Then, among the mausoleums and moss-covered tombs, I see him again.

Uncle Ray.

The statue does not look the same. A drastic change from what I saw earlier today, he stands regal, yet frightened. In this dim lighting the years of wear are barely noticeable. I wish I had brought my camera, but I know that to be disrespectful, especially this evening when we have so much to accomplish.

He stands frozen in time, arms outstretched, and face locked in a grimace of terror. His mouth is gaped open, each detail of his petrified form, a testament to his final, anguishing moments. He stands before me, as he did this afternoon, in dreams and during the séance, however, this evening, cast in the night's glow, he seems almost alive. My chest tightens as I reach out to touch his cold stone face, tracing my hand down to his outstretched arm. Looking upon his tortured form, in a solemn voice I whisper, "As I promised, we are here to release you, and to bring peace to all who are in torment here."

Behind me, Madam Claire begins her work. Wishing I could help, but not knowing how, I can only watch as she spreads a blanket a short distance away while carefully placing the box in its center. Her voice rises in a melodic chant, words in Creole I am not meant to know, yet can feel deep within my bones. She circles the statue, sprinkling salt from one pocket and ash from another, each movement precise and meaningful. The wind tangles with the Spanish moss hanging from the old oak tree, causing it to sway and bristle softly as if the elements themselves were answering her call. The air pulses in rhythm with her chant.

A symphony of sound grows around us. The rustling of leaves, the mournful wail of the wind through the moss, and what sounds like faint voices, singing a haunting chorus. The melody emanates from the earth, the stones and even from the stars above.

Madam Claire turns to me, her eyes steady and sure.

She pulls gently at my sleeve. "Come, child," she says, her voice low but firm.

I kneel beside her on the damp ground, the grass cold and wet against my knees. She takes my hand, her touch grounding me as she guides my other hand to rest on the icy shoe of Uncle Ray's petrified form. The moment I touch it, a strange warmth courses through me, as though the stone itself is alive and listening.

"Believe, child," she urges, her gaze piercing yet kind.

"Speak dese words cher, from a place of peace, an' wit' a forgivin' heart." Speak yo uncle's name, speak Saphron's name, an' wit' extreme forgiveness, speak Celeste's name. Let our family's spirits find peace. Let us find peace."

I hesitate, my voice caught somewhere between fear and determination. I feel Madam Claire's unwavering support and belief in me and something deep inside shifts. My confidence grows and I now accept that I belong here. It is now that I truly understand the importance of my role in this ritual. From behind me, Madam Claire speaks in a guarded accent, one I have never heard come from her before. The phrases she utters sound like an ancient language. Softly, repeatedly and melodically, she sings with conviction, words no other outsider has ever heard before.

I instinctively know it is time for me to perform my portion of this ritual.

"Uncle Ray," I say, my throat tightening as I picture his anguish.

"Saphron." I can feel her life's light as it brushes against me.

"Celeste." A wave of pain and sorrow surges through me at the thought of her betrayal, but I speak with genuine forgiveness in my heart.

"Let our family's souls find solace. Let us all at last find peace."

As the last phrase leaves my lips, the restless air swirling around us slows to a still, as if the cemetery itself awaits her family's restless spirit's permission to breathe again. Then the wind suddenly roars, carrying Madam Claire's chants into the night. Shadows shift, coalescing around the statue. My body begins to quake as shapes emerge, ghostly figures, their faces pale echoes of the living. I recognize them from photos on Madam Claire's mantel. Family members long gone, unwitting victims of a curse spoken on this spot fifteen years ago. Their eyes are hollow, their expressions a mixture of sorrow, yearning, and torment.

"Stay back," Madam Claire warns, her voice cutting through the rising wind.

"Their pain must end tonight."

I watch, paralyzed, as the spirits move closer, encompassing the statue. Madam Claire's chants weave through the air, binding the restless souls to the ritual. The wind howls, the moss glistens, and the clouds part just enough to reveal the faint light of the moon. The cemetery comes alive with energy. Before us an unseen force vibrates through the gravestones causing the tall grass to sway. Apparitions dance in the night, almost joyously in appreciation of our efforts to bring closure to all.

Finally, the ritual reaches its climax. Madam Claire kneels before the statue, her voice softening as she speaks words I cannot understand, but I know they are final. A brilliant light suddenly bursts from the center of the circle she drew on the ground, reaching past the clouds and stars, illuminating the cemetery in an unworldly glow. The spectral figures which have been swirling around my uncle slow to a halt. Their forms separate into individual streams of light and ascend into the night sky just above the marbled statue of Uncle Ray. Once together, their auras look down upon Madam Claire in reverence and thanks.

Their features blurred in the spectral light; we see two separate apparitions a slight distance from the others. The first is the daughter of Madam Claire, and the second Saphron. They reach out as if to ask to join with their ancestors. We watch with jubilant hearts as their essences move slowly towards the open arms of the others, becoming one once again with all family members. Once all souls are united, the wind dies down in approval, leaving a profound silence in its wake. Now one brilliant orb of light, the once restless spirits join with the bright light emanating from the circular portal Madam Claire drew earlier. They have found their much-deserved peace.

Elated for Madam Claire's family, I am concerned the chants and talismans have done nothing to help my uncle gain his freedom. My concerns are soon washed away as the soil beneath my feet shakes.

A sound like no other, a deep, guttural wail rises from the very bowels of the earth, echoing beneath us. We watch as the statue of Uncle Ray trembles, moving slightly from side to side. Light rushes through cracks forming along the stone's surface, blinding me momentarily. Then, an unearthly hiss precedes a loud cracking sound. Madam Claire and I stand motionless.

"Release him," she says quietly as the statue crumbles to the ground, coming to rest at our feet.

In front of us, we see a glowing form, the spirit of my uncle, whose soul is free at last. Hovering before us is a translucent silhouette. Trying to keep a tight grip on my emotions, a tear streams down my cheek as he turns to me, his eyes filled with gratitude.

I hear an inaudible voice deep within my mind, and recognize it to be his, "Thank you, both for your courage and forgiveness."

Knowing this will be my last time communicating with him, my mind searches for the right words, but before I can find them, Uncle Ray's form gently transforms into a brilliant stream of light. I watch in awe as he rises, joining the others who are patiently waiting above. There are no words that can ever fully capture the sense of joy, peace, and pure bliss that now fills the night sky and our hearts. Together, through love and forgiveness, the burdens of two families are finally lifted, and in their place, healing can at last begin to blossom, offering a new chapter of hope and renewal.

Madam Claire places a hand on my shoulder. "It is done."

"He thanked us," I say with a relieved sigh.

"I know dear, I heard him too."

The orb of light above fades into the night, leaving behind an air of love and serenity.

I look up at the sky now clear and dotted with stars. A strange calm settles over me. With the curse now broken, and the tormented souls finally set free, a sense of peace blankets Madam Claire's family's plot. And though some questions linger about the past, and we remain unclear about what the future may hold, I know one thing for certain, tonight, we have rewritten both our family's stories.

From pain comes peace, and from darkness, light.

Home Again, but Haunted

Back in Cincinnati, I am caught between worlds, the one I know and the one I stumbled into in New Orleans. My article is due in a week, but the real challenge is not writing it but rather explaining to my mother what happened.

I found Uncle Ray, her brother. But how do I tell her he spent the last fifteen years as a statue, cursed by an angry voodoo priestess? It sounds ludicrous, even to me, and I was there. I have photos of the statue, each uncanny in their resemblance to Uncle Ray, down to his signature Columbo coat and fedora. But convincing Mom of the truth feels impossible.

From the phone call I made to her, I can tell mom is not looking forward to me coming for a visit today.

We sit at her dining room table, the heart of what used to be our family home. I have laid out my case, spreading it over the table. Before us are my notes, photographs, and Uncle Ray's tattered journal. Her fingers hover over them, reluctant to touch.

"Why couldn't you just let this go?" she asks, her voice a

mix of sorrow and frustration.

"I needed to know what happened to him," I reply. "To bring closure, for you, for me, for all of us."

"Closure?" she scoffs, holding up the second draft of my article.

"This is pure fiction; these are tall tales, Eddie. If you publish this, you'll be laughed right out of Cincinnati."

Her disbelief stings, but I do not flinch. Pointing to my photo evidence I reiterate, "But, Mom, look at the statue. Look at the coat and the hat! You can't deny it is him."

She shakes her head, resolute. "A coincidence, that's all. I could find a dozen statues online that look like him. That doesn't mean they are your uncle."

Desperation bubbles up inside me. I know what I am about to say will change everything, but I cannot hold in my frustration any longer.

"What about Uncle Michael?" I ask, my voice soft but deliberate.

Her eyes narrow, "What about him?"

"He wasn't our uncle," I say, meeting her gaze. "He was Uncle Ray's boyfriend. Uncle Ray told me as much himself when his spirit visited me."

My words hang in the air. Mom stares at me, her mouth slightly open, unable to speak.

"I know how this sounds," I continue, my voice trembling. "But it's the truth. Uncle Ray's soul was trapped in that stony hell. Mom, he told me things only our family would know. Things about his life, about Michael, and about you."

I can sense how badly mom wants me to stop talking. She, like the rest of the family chose to never acknowledge that Uncle Ray was gay, and for me to have the nerve to bring it up now seems disrespectful to her.

"He was angry with his partner," I continue, "they broke up. Now, I don't really remember Micheal well, but I know he came over several times after Uncle Ray came up missing. You always sent us to play in our rooms when he visited. Well, Uncle Ray was upset about their break-up, so hurt that he wanted to get revenge on Micheal for breaking his heart. In New Orleans, he learned about voodoo and began to believe in it. To learn how to use it, he took advantage of a young and naive girl named Saphron and broke her heart. She died the night he was forced to confront her about ending their friendship. He said he'd been cursed by Saphron's mother, Celeste, to stand watch over her grave forever."

Realizing I have struck a nerve, I should end our conversation there but cannot. "Mom, how would I know these facts? You certainly have not shared any of this with me. Can you deny what I am saying is true?"

Mom stands and slaps the tabletop yelling, "Why do you insist on telling me this!?"

"Because mom, when I was down there, I too, did not believe in all that hocus pocus, but I ran into someone, and she helped me understand things. She wanted to settle all the bad blood between our families. She told me one family member from each side, with forgiveness in their hearts, would allow the curse to be lifted. I know mom, all this sounds unreal. I thought so too until I became involved in it. Once I understood and believed, I was glad to help release him. And now he's free and at peace."

Her silence is deafening. Knowing mom the way I do, I realize this conversation is over, so I gather the photos, the journal, and my notes, attempting to protect myself against her doubt.

"I'm writing the article," I say, my tone firm but gentle. "I wish you could believe me. I know how hard that is mom, but why would I make up such a story? I wish, if nothing else, you could accept that Uncle Ray is finally in heaven because I was there and able to help set him free."

Mom does not respond. Her eyes glisten as she holds back tears. I see a mixture of anger, disbelief, and something else I cannot quite place. Maybe, just maybe, a faint crack in her certainty.

I leave her sitting at the dining room table and before leaving out the front door I yell, "I love you mom, maybe we can talk some more next week."

No response.

To be honest, I do not know if mom will ever believe me.

Even today it is hard for me to fully accept what I experienced was real. But I lived it and witnessed the impossible. Whether anyone else believes it, Uncle Ray's story deserves to be told.

I will take the risk and make sure it is published because some stories are too strange and powerful to stay buried. I know this article reads as if it were drafted by a madman. I also accept the reality that our editor may laugh me out of the building. I will not allow anything or anyone to stop me from letting readers get to know about my Uncle Ray and the terrible fate he suffered at the hands of Celeste. I will go to every magazine and newspaper until I find one willing to print this story.

If those efforts fail, I may be forced to write a book regarding the epic saga of a reporter who vanished while visiting New Orleans, a historical and mysterious place known to capture not only the hearts, but also the souls of the people who dare visit.

The Weight of the Truth

The harsh glow of the computer screen washes over me as I stare at the blinking cursor. The words in my mind feel heavy, as though they carry the weight of more than just this story. This article is no longer just an anniversary piece. I am recording my uncle's life and legacy, or what remains of it. His final days, bound by mysteries and curses, bring me to write an epic saga I am not sure even happened. I find myself still struggling to believe the things I witnessed and survived.

I have no one else to blame for the mess in which I find myself. That Friday, over a month ago, I was so cocky and confident I could spin a poignant narrative about a reporter lost to time, that I marched into the editor's office, practically begging him to allow me to write this article. The chilling truth, still hidden from my boss, is how far down the rabbit hole of voodoo I allowed myself to go. How am I to explain a journey filled with strange and unsettling sights that haunt me even now, all in my desperate search for Uncle Ray? No one, including me, may ever know the true cost of bringing this story back to Cincinnati.

How do I write about voodoo curses without sounding like a lunatic? How do I tell readers that my uncle was not just lost, that the vengeance of a grieving mother transformed and imprisoned him?

I tap the journal on my desk, its worn leather cover fraying at the edges. Ray's notes and thoughts seemed scattered and often cryptic, but they led me step by step through the city he loved and the horrors he stumbled into. His voice came alive on those pages, describing a vibrant, chaotic New Orleans full of life, intrigue, history, tradition and a darker side which captivated him and eventually led to his tragic demise.

I lean back in my chair, rubbing my temples. Scattered across my desk are my notes and recordings. I pick up the pictures taken of the statue. The images of the figure bear an uncanny resemblance to Uncle Ray as he stands frozen in marbled agony, but like my mother, others may believe that those pictures could represent anyone. I have recordings of Madam Claire's raspy voice recounting the spells her daughter used to cast upon my uncle that vengeful curse. But even with all this evidence, who could believe such an outlandish tale? A narrative so strange that it borders on the absurd. *Could I convince our editor?* I think to myself. *Not likely, but I must try.* I know this much to be true, I will be broke repaying the expense account should the editor decide to kill the story.

But I must write something. Not just to cover my ass financially, but for my Uncle Ray, the man who let his curiosity and ambition destroy him, leaving his family in shambles. Do I focus on a man whose soul I freed in a cemetery under a moonlit sky alongside a voodoo priestess? Or will I craft an article around a man lost to the world, a mystery that remains unsolved, leaving lingering suspicion and unresolved grief?

I have a few days to decide which avenue to take regarding this anniversary article. Common sense tells me to tear up the draft I showed mother and to choose the subject which will leave my uncle's disappearance unsolved. My heart, however, leans towards a narrative most, if not all readers will consider no more than a fictional recounting of a story that never happened. For any reasonable person this is a straightforward choice, especially if I intend to work as a reporter in this town again.

The Article

It has been four days, and I have finally come up with a draft to hand into my editor. With the article's publication uncertain, the ominous possibility of unemployment looms over me. With one last chance to rework it, I decide to take what I have home for one final polish.
The fan of the laptop hums as the blank page awaits my words.

To stop the blinking curser, I type:

Ray Lybarger, Beloved Missing Reporter Found

Fifteen years ago, Ray Lybarger disappeared while chasing a story. What he found instead was a curse that bound him to New Orleans in ways he never fathomed. This is not the story I intended to write, but it's the only one I can.

There you have it, I think, staring at the first paragraph and daring it to challenge me. *Choice made, there can be no going back now.*

A Night I'll Never Forget

There's a certain magic in New Orleans, a pulse you can feel beneath the music-filled streets, in the shadowy corners of old cemeteries, and under the sprawling arms of ancient oaks. The city keeps its secrets hidden to most, but on one foggy night, I stumbled onto a story so deeply woven into the city's fabric that I may never fully untangle it.

This is the story of my uncle, Ray Lybarger.

He has been gone for 15 years. Well, that is what my family believed. But a series of events I could never have predicted led me to a handmade talisman, a mysterious voodoo priestess named Madam Claire, and an above-ground cemetery bathed in eerie moonlight shrouded in mystery.

I went to New Orleans searching for answers, but what I found was beyond anything I imagined.

The Cemetery of Secrets

That night the air was heavy with the scent of moss, damp leaves and the faint sweetness of wilting flowers. Madam Claire stood before a weathered old statue, her voice low and melodic as she chanted in a language I did not understand. I clutch an amulet hung loosely around my neck, prayed over by this woman to protect and calm me.

"You must believe my child," Madam Claire explained. "We are dealing with forces beyond ourselves."

I would come to understand that my uncle's soul became trapped in his stony prison by forces he could not comprehend and that his very essence was bound there, unable to move, cursed to watch over a graveside he could never leave. This article is to help you, my readers, comprehend what occurred and share with me a night that would change me forever.

The voodoo priestess and I were in that above ground cemetery to perform a ritual. One designed to release not just one, but many souls that night.

This is the part of the article where you, as my reader says, this cannot be real. I am here to tell you; it is a moment I will never forget

Unable to help, I could only watch as she spread ash and salt on the ground surrounding us, her voice, melodic yet forceful. A hushed reverence enveloped me as I stood by her side, finally understanding and accepting my intricate part in this ritual.

When the spell reached its crescendo, and his soul was set free, the fog seemed to pull inward, swirling toward the grave where my uncle's statue stood. Low and tired was his voice as he spoke, yet not out loud. I became uneasy as his words were disembodied yet clear as they entered directly into my consciousness, bypassing my ears entirely.

I hear three whispered words. *"I am free."*

I stood frozen as Uncle Ray's translucent figure appeared before me, his eyes reflecting a mixture of sorrow and gratitude. "I made mistakes," I hear echoing in my mind, his voice carrying a weight I could feel in my chest. *"Please nephew, don't let my story end with bitterness."*

He looked at me with a kindness I have never known before in life. *"Tell them,"* he urges me, *"about this place, its beauty, and its history. Warn them certain secrets are best left unknown lest they unleash unforeseen consequences. Some traditions, my dear nephew, will always demand respect."*

And then, just as quickly as he had appeared, he was gone.

What Does It All Mean?

I have replayed that night in my mind countless times. If you would have asked me a month ago if I believed in spirits, voodoo, dark magic and the occult, I too would have laughed. But now I cannot say for certain.

What I do know is that New Orleans transcends the definition of a city. It is more than a place to live and visit, it is a living, breathing entity with its own unique rhythm and soul, and a place where history and modernity collide. The Crescent City's traditions, people, and history all demand our respect.

Eddie Schmitt

Contributing Reporter for the *Cincinnati Enquirer*

Well, there it is, in black and white. A story so strange and unbelievable that I again doubt myself. Yes, this is truly an odd and unusual tale. It would behoove me to rethink handing it in. The stubborn German side of me will not allow me to second guess my choice. *No sense arguing with yourself, you have made your decision, now live with it.* Sometimes, I wish for the ability to shut my mind and consciousness down.

My deadline is today, and I just got word our editor is out ill. In a weird sense, I feel the powers that be are being very kind allowing me to place my article on his desk and make a hasty retreat. Because of this wonderful happenstance I have no fear of being called into his office later this afternoon for having written an article no one would ever believe.

I cross my fingers and say a prayer to Uncle Ray, "Hope I did you proud, and I hope this doesn't get me fired."

Before leaving the building for the day, I pen a letter to my editor in hopes it will help him better understand why I decided to hand in this practically unbelievable article.

Dear Sir,

Whether you believe my account or not, I hope this article will prompt both you and my readers to ask questions about the world around us, and to look at New Orleans with a bit more wonder and reverence. There are mysteries within The Crescent City and the French Quarter that remain unspoken, their secrets concealed in shadows, waiting to be discovered.

Some stories shift our perspective, revealing hidden meanings and unexpected connections. This is the lesson I carry with me from my experience in New Orleans. All I ask is that you and our readers approach this article with an open mind. Each day presents new possibilities, and some experiences, no matter how unbelievable to someone else, can leave you forever changed.

That night, in the bitter cold air of an above-ground cemetery, I was forced to accept things I once considered absurd. Because of that experience, I had the honor of witnessing something you may not believe, but I assure you, it happened. The events I experienced have profoundly impacted the way I view life and my fellow man.

Though submitting this article may put my job at risk, it is a chance I must take. If only one person finds belief in something greater than themselves through my uncle's story, it will have been worth it.

I will never again question anyone's faith, nor take for granted any religion, especially voodoo, which I was fortunate to watch in action through the skill and devotion of a remarkable woman, whose trust and grace have forever transformed me.

With tear-filled eyes, I watched in awe as my uncle's soul was released from the torment that bound him. Through faith, belief, and powers beyond my understanding, I witnessed him attain his freedom. Because I did not close my mind, heart, and soul to new possibilities, he is now able to rest in peace, beneath the Creole stars.

www.ingramcontent.com/pod-product-compliance
Lightning Source LLC
Chambersburg PA
CBHW060328310726
48976CB00007B/2485